SECRETS OF AN

UNFAITHFUL

LOVER

2

KANDY KAINE

Acknowledgements

First and foremost, I want to honor God. He is the head of my life and my family. Without him there would be no me. Many nights I have prayed to him and he has never failed me yet. I also want to say thank you to all my readers, supporters, friends and family. Without all of you none of this would be possible. I never thought I would be writing more books. When Revenge Takes Over 1&2 did good. As well as Obsessed With My Boss. Secrets Of An Unfaithful lover part one was amazing, I hope you enjoy part two as well. I'm glad that everybody is enjoying my style of writing. I want to thank all the people who thought that I wouldn't make it in this industry by doubting me. Even though this industry is tough to break into, I will do my best to continue to write great books for everyone to read. I hope everyone enjoys this book as well as others to come. Thanks for being a part of my new journey.

Dedications:

I dedicate this book to myself. I worked so hard to make this book come alive. I worked long and hard to ensure that this series was better than my last. To my amazing girlfriend AJ, I just want to say thank you for being my number one supporter. You have stuck it out with me even when I wanted to quit. I also want to tell you how much I love you for continuing to show your love and support every day. To my boys, Kindall and Kamron I'm writing these books for you both, so that the both of you know not to stop something that you started. As well as; anything is possible if you just put your minds to it. To my mother I want to say thank you for telling me not to give up. Also, for supporting me in everything I do, I love you. I also want to thank my readers/supporters who love to engage in a very good book. We can only go up from here. Without all of you I would not be able to keep going.

SHOUT OUTS:

I would like to give a special shout out to a few people who has helped me through this book. Courtney Dee, thank you for making my book come alive with my amazing covers you made for me. A few more are Chantel Williams, Tiffany Gilbert, Nichole Jackson, Sherri Marie, Ashantay Keys-Titus, Louis Haynes, Chanique Jones, Glenda Jackson. Thanks all of you for keeping me focused on my talent and not quitting.

<u>Synopsis:</u>

Ж

It's funny how your past has a way of catching back up to you; when you least expect it to. Victoria thought that if she kept everything from her fiancé, that it would go away; she couldn't have been more wrong. Her bones are falling from her closet a lot quicker than she wanted. She soon realizes that she has bitten off more than she can chew. She's gone from stalking to getting pregnant. But nothing could change her mind from being faithful to Collin. But suspicions are raised with Victoria never wanting to be home, as well as his parents' home being invaded. With Victoria's last year of school being around the corner, she is faced with another decision that will make a big impact on her life. That is, stay where she is, or move to the states. There's so much to gain with moving to the states, but she could also stand to lose Collin. With so much on her plate, she is still sleeping around. She becomes the victim of many addictions far worse than sex. With her mother no longer there to be a shoulder to cry on, she tries to find a way to cope. Will she earn her life back, or will she lose herself in the lies and secrets that she refuses to change? They say that the truth will set you free. Will she get her freedom, or remain a prisoner in her own web of lies?

Previously In Part One:

Ж

I text Mario to make sure he was still meeting with me today at the hotel, but he changed the location on me; he wanted me to meet him at the beach, I was confused. What the hell did he have up his sleeves now? Every time we pick a place to meet up at now, he always changes it. After getting dressed I made sure that Collin was far away from me before I made my phone call to the doctor.

"Follow me to the beach house and I will get the money for you," he demanded closing my door and walking off.

The last time we went to his beach house we ended up having sex. We had to have been there for a couple of days, but what was scaring me was why he stashed his money at the beach house? I haven't been getting anymore phone calls from his wife, but that was neither here or there. She was a sneaky woman and I'm pretty sure she knows that I was still seeing her husband. Pulling off and slowly following behind his car. In the back of my mind I knew we wasn't just going to his place just to pick up the money, but I needed it. I had to have this abortion one way or another. As we pulled up to his place my phone rang; it was Collin.

"Hello," I answered.

"Hey baby, how was your doctor's appointment?"

"It was ok. I just have to take some meds for a stomach virus. I should be home soon. I'm picking up a few things. Did you need anything while I am out?" I had to say something that wouldn't raise suspicion.

"Ok baby. I will see you when you get home. I Love you baby."

"I love you too," I said before hanging up the phone.

As soon as I did Mario was at my passenger door rushing me to get out. Getting out the car I swear I saw Quan standing across the street staring at me, but when I turned around to look nobody was there; that guy is creepy. Only had sex with him twice and he has not left me alone since. Walking into Mario's house noticing that he had moved a lot of things around.

"Are you moving or something?" I asked being nosey.

"No, just doing some spring cleaning. Come to the back room with me the money is in my safe."

As we walked to his room that was in the far back of the house. The smell of bleach and other household cleaners filled the air. It was spotless in here since the last time we were here. The bed was made up perfectly, but the paint on the walls were not finished. I would have rather went to the hotel today because the different smells were making me sick to my stomach. I covered my nose and sat down on the bed.

"So, you keep all your loose cash here?" I asked to at least get him talking. He was way too quiet for me.

"No, I did a little run with some of my friends and came up on some cash. Why, are you a spy or something? Are you going to turn me in?" I started to laugh at him. Even though he got on my nerves at times he still made me smile. I just hope he don't change his mind. Times like this I wish that I wasn't with Collin and he didn't have a wife. I wanted him so much I wanted him all to myself.

"Yeah, and I will be handcuffing you and taking you in. So, are you really going to give me the money, so I can get my car fixed?" I had to put the attention back on what I was there for.

"Speaking of the money. Tell me the real reason why you need it because I know damn well it's not for your car. You just bought that mother fucker when I gave you some money. What you think I didn't know? I know everything that you do." I looked at him in fear. Not knowing what was going to happen next, I got up off the bed and headed for the door. "Where the hell do you think you're going? I'm not fucking done talking to you!" he yelled. I flinched and rushed back in his room.

"I was just going to use the bathroom Mario. What the hell is wrong with you?"

"You must think I'm stupid. Or maybe you think I don't know what the hell is going on."

He walked closer to me and the next thing I knew Mario had his hands wrapped around my neck. I couldn't believe what I was feeling. He was enraged with anger. Sweat was dripping down his beard. This was not like him and I had no clue why he was acting the way he was acting. What felt like forever he had a tight grip on my neck for about a few seconds then he let me go. I didn't even scream because it just made me horny.

"Where did that come from?" I asked him, holding onto my throat.

"Take all your fucking clothes off!"

"Ok, I have been wanting you to fuck me real good daddy." I took off my clothes nice and slowly. Sliding back onto the bed he shut the door and locked it. That was new to me. He never locked the door. He lunged towards me and began to go crazy.

"You didn't think I was going to find out that you were pregnant? My eyes went wide. "I told you a long time ago bitch that you were mine. And you go around and get pregnant by some dumb ass scum bag?"

"Let me go Mario!" I yelled. "You don't know what you're talking about!"

"Victoria, you must think I'm stupid. Your breast are bigger, and your hips are wider. Now who the fuck are you pregnant by?"

"Nobody!" Who the hell was he talking to? How in the hell did he know I was even pregnant? I'm not even showing.

"Ok, well I'm about to make sure!"

Mario face went from normal to red in a split second. Again, he wrapped his left hand around my neck and with his right he pulled off his pants. Lying there with fear in my eyes he firmly inserted his dick inside me. It was not like any other time we had sex. It was more anger behind it and force. I tried to break free from him telling him that he was hurting me, but he was not hearing me at all. It was like he was in another world.

"Mario! Stop please your hurting me!" I yelled. He just kept going. I started to feel a sharp pain in my stomach

14

and back. I yelled out again. "Mario! Please you are hurting me you have to stop!"

"Shut up! I will stop when I'm finished," he yelled back.

I just laid there until he got finished. When he did I ran straight to the bathroom and locked the door behind me. I curled up behind the door and began to cry. I was in so much shock that I didn't notice the blood that was running down my legs. I was in so much pain that I couldn't get back up off the floor. Mario began banging on the door. Curling up I just knew something else bad was going to happen. I could feel my body getting weaker and weaker. The next thing I knew I was on the floor not able to move at all. *"Lord please get me off this floor. Something is wrong, and it feels like my insides are tearing apart. Please God if I never needed you before I need you now."*

<u>Prelude</u>

<u>Ж</u>

Waking up in a hospital room with lights and doctors hovering over me was more than enough to scare me. Not sure what was going on and how I got here raised suspicion. The last thing that I remembered was meeting Mario. I don't remember much that happened after Mario and I had our fight, but I did notice something different. It felt like I had been hit by a car. My body was weak, and I could barely move. Opening my eyes wanting to know what was going on. The nurses continued to poke at me and talk over my head.

"What happened? Why am I here?" I asked the nurse who was taking my vitals.

"Ma'am you were brought into the hospital by officer Shabez. He said that you were badly injured." In the back of my mind I was confused as to why he would bring me and not call the paramedics.

"Oh, he did? Who is that anyway?" I said playing dumb.

"Yeah, he's a really great officer. There are a few things I want to talk to you about. Were you aware that you were almost three months pregnant?"

"Yeah, I had just found out that I was pregnant a few days ago."

"Well, I don't want to be the one who gives you the bad news but, I'm sorry to tell you that you've loss the baby."

An overwhelmed feeling came over my body. I was happy that she said I was no longer pregnant. Just didn't want it to happen the way it did. Mario had made me miscarry and he somehow knew that I was with child. Looking up at the nurse I faked a sad face like I was upset at the bad news. That was one huge secret that I was taking to my grave. The risk of having Collin find out would have been the end of me.

"How did I lose it?" I asked just so that they wouldn't raise suspicion?"

"Well, from the looks of it you had some hemorrhaging and some trauma in the abdomen. Were you fighting with anyone; or did you fall?"

"No, I just remember going to the beach and then I woke up here. I am in a lot of pain."

"Ok we will come back and check up on you in a bit. You did lose a lot of blood, so we are going to keep you here for a while. Just to make sure that you're ok to go home. Is there anybody you want me to call and let them know that you're here?"

"No, I really don't want to see anyone, nor let anyone know what's going on."

"Are you sure? At times like this family are the best ones to make you feel better." I just shook my head and turned away. "Get some rest." She patted my leg and walked out with the other nurses.

Laying there in so much pain I still couldn't believe that Mario was the cause of this. But the crazy part about it was I still loved him. Call me crazy, but he had every right to be mad. I promised him that I wouldn't get pregnant or have sex with anybody but him. That was easier said than done. I was addicted to sex, and I couldn't just have one man.

I wasn't in my right mind or I was really doped up because all I could think about was leaving the hospital and going to see Treyvon. At a time like this I should have been wanting to get better, but I just didn't want to be alone. Collin would have been asking me all kinds of questions instead of making sure I was ok. After a while I started to feel really sleepy. Not sure how long I was going to be in here. I just closed my eyes and hoped I woke up from this horrible dream.

Chapter One: Present Day

Ж

Today was going to be the longest day ever. A couple of days ago I had received a call from one of my mother's friends telling me that my mother had been in the hospital for the past couple of months. When I received the news, I didn't believe it. My mother always let me know when something was wrong. I didn't understand why she didn't want to tell me what she was going through. All these years trying to stay away from her, she really needed me.

Since I was all my mother had I had to be the one who was in charge to do everything for her funeral. With the help of Collin and his parents, I felt a little bit of relief. It still wasn't clicking in my head that she was gone until I went to see her in the morgue. She was so pale and when I touched her body it was cold as ice and stiff. The picture of her was stained in my mind even after I left.

For the very first time in my life I thought about someone other than myself. I hadn't talked to any of my male friends, nor went to see them. A couple of times I got a few messages from Treyvon, but I just ignored it. I couldn't handle any of them at this point, or so I thought. It was like my body was reacting in a way that made my hormones even worse. I snuck to see Treyvon two days ago, and now I want him more and more. He let me cry on his shoulder for hours before we had sex. I know at this time I'm supposed to be grieving, but it was like something came over me.

This morning I woke up with an uneasy feeling in my chest. I was not ready to burry my mother, just like I was not ready to burry my father. Anybody who has lost a parent would understand the pain and emptiness that I feel inside. Not only have I lost my mother, but my father as well. I was the only child so now it was just me. Keeping my mind from going crazy I just prepared to go to my mother's funeral. Collin and his parents made sure that I was ok, but he knew it was bothering me. As he got ready he tried his best to make me feel better.

"Hey babe, I set your dress out for you to ware today," he said trying his best to be supportive.

"I saw it, that's not the dress I wanted to ware," I replied.

"Well, I was only trying to be helpful."

"I don't need you picking out my clothes!" I snapped. He was being really annoying today. He never dressed me after this long, why start now?

"Look, I know you just lost your mom, but you need to calm down. I am here for you, but you are not going to talk to me like that!"

"Whatever, I can take care of myself. I don't need your help dressing me Collin!"

"You need to stop. I know you are upset right now but you are tripping."

I don't know what came over me, but a deep wave of rage and pain came over me. Collin was only trying to be there for me and I snapped. All this time I could have spent with my mom, I didn't. I was too worried about making myself happy, and getting my needs met. I hated myself. Collin walked out the beach house and went to make sure his parents were ready. My mother's ceremony was in an hour, and I was not at all prepared. As I began to finish getting ready Collins mother came in.

"Hey sweetie, is everything ok?" she asked grabbing my hand. Tears started running down my face.

"I miss my mom. Why didn't she tell me that she was sick? I could have helped her."

"Right now, is not the time to think about what you could have done. Your mother loved you and still loves you. You must pull yourself together Victoria. Now wipe your face, she is very proud of you sweetie and so am I. You are a part of our family now, and we will love you just as much as she did. I'm going to make sure everyone else is ready. Everything will be ok."

"Yes, ma'am."

Getting myself in the right mind we headed to the church where my mothers' funeral would be held. The streets were filled with people who was either just passing by or had known that it was a funeral today. As we arrived the entrance to the church was blocked. People was going in and leaving flowers and chanting prayers. It was making it even harder for me to believe that it was my mother who was in that church.

"Everything will be ok." Collin assured me before we got out the car.

"I know, I still can't believe this is real." With my phone on silent I placed it in my purse and got out the car. I didn't want anyone texting me while I was laying my mother to rest.

We headed up the stairs hand and hand with his parent's right behind us. All around us were people praying and crying. I wasn't sure if they knew my mother, but it warmed my heart that they were here. When I walked in, I could barely walk; Collin had to hold me up so that we could go to the front of the church. I couldn't even look at her in that state. Collin and I sat down as others went to see her for the last time. Once everyone was settled the pastor began to speak.

"Heavenly father. We are gathered here today to send Mrs. Valorie home to you. She has been here on this earth as a child of yours to do your great works. She was a great leader at her job and an amazing mother to her daughter. She is now able to accompany her husband

Roberto and be free from this world we call home. We are happy that she was able to go in ease, and not suffer from any pain. All of her friends are here to say their last goodbyes to her. Valorie you will be deeply missed. I would like to take this time to ask Victoria to come and speak about her mother."

In the pit of my stomach I could feel everything inside of me turning. I didn't know what to say about my mother. We hadn't talked in a while before she passed. Feeling like I failed her, I didn't think how I felt really mattered. I looked over at Collin as he nudged me to get up from my seat to go speak. Finally getting up the courage. I stood in front of all my mother's friends I never knew she had. I just said how I felt so I could get it over with.

"I never thought that my mother would leave me like this. Even though we didn't see eye to eye, she still was an amazing woman. I had a feeling something was wrong with her for years, but she would never say what.

Finding out that my mother died from cancer and she didn't tell me hurts the most, but I know that she is no longer suffering. For years it was just me and her because we lost my dad while he was on duty. Knowing that they are back together warms my heart. It just about killed my mother when he passed. Mom I want you to know that I love you so much and I will mis you. I wish I was able to tell you how much you meant to me before you passed. I want to let you know that I graduated. I know how much you wanted me to finish school and I did. I also want to let you know that I will not let you down. I will make you and daddy proud of me. I can't see my life on this earth without you, so I know my life will get harder. You were the world not just to me, but to everyone. I want to tell you that I am sorry for all of the pain that I caused you."

After that I couldn't speak any more. My eyes began to overflow with tears. Collin came to get me and walked me out the church. I took one last look at my mother laying still in her casket. Flowers were all around her. Everyone started to get up and place more flowers around her. I never imagined that my mother would get so much love as she did. Even the officers that served with my father were present. Overwhelmed and heartbroken I couldn't fight back the tears. How could I let her die alone? Collin and his family were standing right beside me. When I looked up again there was Mario. He knew who my parents were, so I wasn't surprised that he came. What I was upset about was the fact he never apologized to me about how he treated me, but today was not the day to care. He walked up to my mom; gave her a flower, spoke to Collins parents and left. That was a big bullet I dodged. That was the last thing I needed was for him to show his ass at my mother's funeral.

In that moment I wanted to pass out. As they closed the casket to take her to her final resting place I lost it. She was all I had, and all I wanted was to make her happy. We followed the young men who were carrying her, so she could be buried. Walking her though the streets of Rio, everyone started to throw her flowers as they sung. I just cried. This was not happening. The beginning of my year was already starting off really rough. After placing her in the ground, I just wanted to go home. I went back to my mother's house and laid in her bed crying; leaving Collin and his parents back at their house. I know that they were worried about me, but I just wanted to be left alone.

Chapter Two: A Month Later

Ж

"Hey baby, I really missed you. Where have you been?" I said to Mario.

"I have been working, what's going on?"

"Nothing, I was just sitting here thinking that we should take a little trip, just the two of us."

"Victoria, you know that I can't do that. I don't have any time off right now. Plus, my wife is really sick. The last time I saw or talk to you I was angry, but hey who could blame me. You got pregnant on me and wanted to hide it."

"Mario look, that was the past. I wasn't pregnant," I still lied to him. "I had a really bad stomach virus. You took me to the hospital and left me, they said. If you cared so much you should have stayed!"

"Well I didn't, what else did you want? I have to get back to work."

"Damn I just wanted to see you, but I guess wifey comes first. When you are done with her call me."

I hung up the phone with a sour taste in my mouth. You would think he would be on my ass after what he did to me. It was cool though, I still had other options. I had to make sure I kept each one of them on my side so that I could continue to live the lavish life I wanted.

Since Collin and I were finished with school, I continued to beg him to move to the states. After what happened to his parents he still won't go. We postponed the wedding until we were sure it was the right time. Honestly, I really don't think it's going to happen. Now that Collin had a new job, he has been acting really funny. When he comes home he acts like I am invisible. When he does that I don't get mad. I just get what I need elsewhere. With him working with his school, he is bringing in major money as a biotech. You wouldn't even think he would be in that field by the way he looked.

After a while Collin started to dress differently, and he grew his hair out even longer. He was buff in his arms, chest and legs. I was drawn to him, but he was not at all engaging with me. I wouldn't put it past him if he had went out and fucked somebody else, hell I would have loved to enjoy that with him. The distance between us was deep, and I wasn't sure still on why he felt the way he did.

Starting my day, I went in to the big house to see if Collins mother had fixed anything for breakfast, and she didn't. So, I went to my favorite place to eat, the pier. Collin was already gone to work, and I didn't even bother to text him. While at the pier, I gotten an alarming text from Quan who still wouldn't leave me alone. After he had threatened to bring harm to Collin and his family I continued to see him. I felt like I was trapped. If I told

Collin, or the police what was going on; Quan would have spoken of the affair we were having.

"Meet me at the Gansway building in thirty minutes, and you better be there before I get there," he said.

"What for?" I asked. I wasn't in the mood for his bull shit today. I just wanted to chill.

"Just do what I said. Don't make me have to tell your little family about us Victoria."

"Why every time I ask why, you always bring up telling my family what we are doing. Did it ever occur to you that I just might have something to do?"

"I don't care about what it is you have or had to do, I said meet me in thirty minutes and that's what I meant."

Quan hung up the phone in my ear before I can get one more word out. I told myself that I was going to get a handle on things, but it had gotten worse. Driving to meet Quan; not only did Collin text me asking me where I was,

Treyvon text me wanting to meet up. I knew I was in over my head, but the money and all the perks that I get are way more worth it. As I pulled up to the Gansway building I noticed Quan was standing right at the entrance. Dreading to get out the car, I grabbed the keys out the ignition and slowly walked towards him.

"What was so important that I had to stop what I was doing just to come to an old run-down building?" He walked up to me fast and grabbed me by the arm. "Come on now is all this necessary?"

"Hurry up before somebody see's us!" he yelled.

I wasn't sure what was about to happen, but he was in a hurry. This building hasn't been used in so many years that spiderwebs were dangling from everywhere. Trying not to let anything that was dirty touch me, I ducked my head. He was still pulling on my arm as we went through this dark place. It was reminding me of the dreams that I was having. I yanked my arm back.

"Where the hell are you taking me Quan?" I asked with fear.

"Just come on, it's not that far."

"I don't care how far it is. I don't want to be down in here. It's too dark and creepy in here."

"Look you are beginning to get on my last nerve. I thought I would come show you my favorite place."

In that moment I knew that things were going to be ok. The further we walked the deeper and deeper we went into this cave like place. Still pulling at my arm, I was getting scared. I couldn't even call anyone on my phone because I didn't have any service. My heart sank. When he stopped he moved over this thin piece of granite. Once it was moved he bent down and walked into the room.

My mouth dropped. This man had a whole little place in this cave. It was small lights hanging from the ceiling, a little pallet on the ground and what looked like dried up flowers placed all over the room. What in the hell was he doing in here? That's when I noticed it, pictures of me were on the pillow and floor behind me. That's when I began to panic.

"Quan what the hell is this?"

"Victoria, I wanted to show you how much I loved you. This place is where I come to think about you. Oh, and get away from my crazy parents."

"Quan I really don't feel right being here. This is a cave, and I don't like to be closed in. Please can we leave?"

"Awe come on now, don't be afraid I got you," he tried to reassure me. I didn't want to tell him off because I knew he was crazy, but if he didn't hurry this up I was darting out of here.

"Well I'm ready to go Quan!" I yelled, and that's when it happened. He snapped on me.

"You stupid ass bitch! I brought you here to show you how much I love you. All you had to do was just listen."

Watching his eyes go from white to red, gave me just enough reason to know that it was not going to go well from here. I turned around facing away from him and grabbed the first big rock that I saw. While he was still spazzing out to himself. I hit him on the top of his head and ran out. I wasn't sure if he was behind me or not, but at that time I didn't care. I ran as fast as I could to my car.

Once I got the car door opened I seen Quan staggering towards me. I put my car in drive and I got the hell away from him. my heart was pounding way to fast I thought I was going to have an heart attack. What in the hell got into him? He knew that it couldn't ever be anything between us, but he just wouldn't leave me alone. Driving home I called Collin to see if he was there, he didn't answer. What the hell did I get myself into? As I pulled up to the house I just sat there and cried. All of this was getting way too much for me. I was really starting to rethink how I was treating Collin, but it was kind of too late to take back all that I have done.

Chapter Three: Surprise

Ж

"Baby wake up. I have a surprise for you," Collin said as he was hovering over me when I opened my eyes.

"What is it Collin? I'm really not in the mood." I still couldn't get over what had happened a few days ago with Quan. "I just want to sleep baby," I told him.

"I just wanted to surprise you. Today is our seven-year anniversary. Don't you remember?"

looking up at him I was shocked and worried. After all these years he still remembered, but I was the one who never cared about it. He had the biggest smile on his face and he was holding a big box and bag in his hands.

"Of course, I remembered baby, I just don't feel good today. What's in the box?"

"Sit up and open it," he said sitting on the bed right next to me.

Grabbing the box out of his hands and the bag, I sat up with a fake smile on my face. The box was wrapped in bows and some red wrapping paper. I was not surprised that he got me a gift, I just really wasn't into the little corny stuff that he did. Flowers and chocolate were not my idea for a gift. Taking the lid off the box inside was some lingerie and some kinky sex toys. I looked up at him with my eyes wide. Was this some type of trick or a joke?

"Awe Collin, what is all this?" I asked scooting closer to him, then giving him a kiss on the lips. "What made you do all this?"

"You have been through so much. I just wanted to show you just how much I love you."

"Awe. That's so nice of you. What's in the bag?" I asked nervously not wanting to open it up.

"Just open it baby. I don't want to spoil the surprise," he replied.

Inside the bag there was some perfume, some chocolates, and a card. When I opened the card, some money fell out and two tickets. When I turned them over they said Miami Florida on them. My mouth dropped, and tears began to fall from my eyes. As I looked up at him he began to shake his head in a yes motion.

"Are these real?" I asked.

"Yes, baby they are real. In two months we both will be going to Florida, but that's not all."

"What do you mean Collin?"

"We are moving to Florida. Just me and you. Mom and dad are moving to another location here in Brazil, but I know how much it meant to you to pursue your career."

I jumped into his arms with joy. I couldn't believe that he was willing to move with me. After all this time me telling him that I wanted to leave Brazil, he finally listened. The only problem that I had was letting go of Mario, and the two others that I was secretly sleeping with. Camron

had left Brazil earlier this year, so he was one less guy that

I had to worry about.

After I finished looking at the gifts that Collin had

given me we went into the big house. His parents were

already gone for the day, so we had the house to ourselves.

I didn't have anything planned and neither did Collin. He

had decided to take off work for the next three days which

was very odd. He never wanted to miss out on his money.

Going into the kitchen I made us something to eat. I

was in the mood for some bacon and eggs, but there were

none in the refrigerator. Instead I made some toast and grits

and cut up some grapefruit and papaya. Collin just ate some

toast and coffee, he wasn't really big on eating in the

mornings. After we both ate I went into the living room and

turned on the television. They were showing one of my

favorite movies. As I began to watch it, my phone rang. It

was Shelby. She hadn't called me since my mother passed so I was eager to speak with her.

"Hey, girl what's up?" I answered anxious to see what she was up to.

"I'm outside of your house come outside," she said sounding sad and worried.

"Is everything ok girl? You sound like you been crying."

"Can you just please come outside Victoria?"

"Yeah, here I come," I said putting on my sandals heading out the front door.

I wasn't sure what was going on, but from the look on her face it wasn't good. Following right behind me was Collin. I was hoping that he had stayed in the house, but of course he had to be nosey. Walking towards her I noticed that Treyvon was sitting in the driver seat of his truck.

"What is going on Shelby?" I asked as she made it to the passenger door.

"Get the fuck out the car Treyvon!" she yelled.

"Man, Shelby your tripping. I told you that nothing was going on between us!" he replied.

"I said get the fuck out the car!" Treyvon got out the car and walked over to the passenger side of his car. "Now Victoria, I'm going to ask you this one fucking time. Are you fucking my man?"

I looked at Collin then I looked at Treyvon. I didn't want to hurt Collin by saying yes, but hell this bitch had the nerve to come to me after all this time. So, I said what any cheating woman would say. I lied to her ass.

"Shelby, your tripping. Why would you think that I'm sleeping with him? I have known him way longer than you and you are my best friend. Don't you think you are being paranoid?"

"Paranoid? Bitch I have seen the messages that you sent him, and I know that you have been to his house because you left your fucking school ID in his room. So, I'm going to ask you one more time if your sleeping with my man, or I'll just beat it out of you!"

Shelby was yelling at the top of her lungs. Treyvon was just standing there quiet. Collin was looking at me waiting for an explanation that I was not at all ready to give him. Telling either of them the truth would crush them. I felt like I was in hell.

"Shelby calm down, I lost my school ID and he must have found it," I said to ease the tension.

"Baby let's just go, this is crazy. You know I wouldn't do nothing like that to you," Treyvon said trying to get her into the car.

"Get the fuck off me Treyvon. You fucking liar, and your fucking my best friend. How would you feel if I was fucking Collin, or some other dude?" When she said that Treyvon's eyes went evil.

"Man, your trippin' Shelby get in the damn car!" he yelled.

She was not trying to hear it. The next thing I knew she was on top of me punching me in my head. I couldn't do nothing but fight her back. I wasn't about to let her fuck up my face. For about twenty minutes we were fighting and scuffling on the ground. Collin and Treyvon pulled her off of me as she was still yelling and screaming. Collin picked me up off the ground and I dusted myself off.

"You nasty bitch, you got a whole man and your sleeping with everybody else. I guess you wasn't going to stop until you had mine too!"

"LET'S GO!" Treyvon yelled at her. Shelby got into the car, but not after she told Collin some information not even I wanted him to know.

"I hope you don't get pregnant again bitch, and I hope next time you don't get an abortion!"

"Really Shelby, that was low," I said looking her dead in her eyes.

"Fuck you bitch," she said while pulling off with Treyvon.

"Pregnant?" Collin asked me. "What is she talking about Victoria?"

"Nothing Collin, let's just go in the house."

He stood there looking at me with anger in his eyes. Dusting myself off again; I was mad as hell at what just transpired. Leading me into the house and sitting on the couch. Collin was way too quiet; so quiet I just knew that he was very upset with me. He had a blank stare in his eyes, like he was staring off in space.

"Victoria, I'm going to ask you one time and one time only. Were you pregnant by me or not?" I wasn't at all prepared to answer that question. I just looked down at my hands contemplating on my answer. "HELLO! DO YOU HEAR ME TALKING TO YOU?"

"Collin, I don't know what you want me to tell you," I replied.

"Where you or were you not pregnant?"

Hesitant to answer I just sat there quiet. Collin got off the couch so fast he wasn't even in the living room anymore. He went out the door and slammed it behind him. I followed him, I didn't want him to hate me. I know what I did was wrong, but I didn't want him to find out like this.

"Baby please come back in the house. It's not what you think it is."

"It's not what I think!" he yelled. "You get into a fight with your best friend over her boyfriend, and it's not what I think. Then she says you were pregnant. How in the hell am I supposed to think?"

"Look I know it sounds messed up, but nothing was going on between me and him." He looked at me with disbelief. He knew I was lying to him.

I had to keep up with the lies. If I came clean about him then I would've had to come clean about the rest of them. I was still sleeping with Mario, but it was not like it used to be since that day we got into that big argument. Collin was still pacing back and forth not saying a word. His eyes were slowly getting red as tears began to fall from his eyes. After a few short minutes. in walked his parents. He quickly wiped his face as if nothing happened and sat down.

"Hey loves, what's going on?" his mother asked greeting us with hugs and kisses. "Is everything ok? Why the long faces?"

"Nothing is wrong mom. We were just having a discussion. Everything is fine," Collin lied. He knew that had he said anything to his parents then we wouldn't hear the end of it.

"Victoria, what is going on?" she asked me.

"Nothing. We were just talking about us moving to the US, right Collin?"

He looked at me with demise in his eyes. I could tell that after today things were going to change. He walked out the house and I went after him. Not turning back as I called out his name, he got into his car. Leaving me right in his tire tracks as he sped away. I knew that this was going to be a major setback for the lifestyle that I craved.

Chapter Four: The Move

Ж

Today was the first day of my new life. Collin and I had finally moved to Miami Florida, just like he promised. We have been here for about three months now. I can honestly say that this was the best move for me. I'm not sure how well Collin will adjust, but it's a lot of new potential money-making opportunities here. I never thought that I would be here, it was like a dream come true.

Miami was beautiful. The air smelled different, and the people here seemed very nice. Our first week here we went out to eat at this small restaurant and it was amazing. I was glad that I wasn't subject to the same things that they gave us in Rio. Collin was feeling a bit home sick though. Miami's air was clear, and the sun was beaming down on us. Just like in Rio everyone had on some shorts, something revealing, and cool. I was falling in love with this place each day.

As the days went by; Collin was having a hard time finding a job, but I on the other hand landed a job as soon as I arrived. I had been in contact with a guy named Kenny who was a modeling agent. I had sent him a bunch of photos and he insisted that we work together. I didn't tell Collin about it because I knew that he would be upset about it, but hell he still isn't really talking to me.

He had a bunch of money saved up to get us a nice house, but the money was going to run out soon. He was beginning to regret moving out here with me, but there was nothing else he could do but go back to Rio. Had he done that then his parents would find out that the relationship we had was falling apart. I kept telling him to become a model too, but he felt like it was degrading. For a while I let him say little things to me, but now I just ignore him.

Waking up this morning with him not even in the bed, I knew today was going to be a crazy day. Everyday he has been getting up after me, but today he was already in the shower. I went to see if he wanted me to join him. As I walked into the foggy bathroom; he had his head pressed against the shower glass.

"Do you mind if I join you?" I asked as I slid open the shower door.

"You know good damn well you don't want to join me. I don't know why you even came in here bothering me," he said with an attitude.

"Well I just figured that you wanted some company."

"It's been two years since we showered together. I don't expect you to do much for me now," he said. "You have really changed."

"So why did you come to Miami with me Collin? If you are not happy with me then maybe I need to go head and find me a place."

"Do what ever you want to do Victoria. Just know if you leave I am going back home and all of the money that I give you and this house will be gone. You will have to find other ways and means to take care of yourself."

"Is that really necessary?"

"Can I please get done with my shower? Please! Any other time you don't bother me, what do you really want Victoria?"

"I was just trying to talk to you. We can't be in the same house and not be cordial?"

"I guess."

I left him still in the shower with soap all over him. As sexy as he was looking standing there with soap suds running down his body, I was getting turned on. But he didn't want to say too much to me, I don't blame him. I only wanted to make our time here as fun as possible, but he still couldn't talk to me. After about twenty minutes he was back in the room getting dressed. I was already dressed

for the day. I had to meet Kenny today so that we could go

over our contract.

Leaving Collin behind with his attitude I called a

cab to come get me. Collin was the only one with a car, so I

had to get around on my own. I waited about thirty minutes

before the cab pulled up in front of the house.

"Hello ma'am you called for a cab?" the driver

asked rolling down his window.

"Yes, and you right on time. I need to go to the

Quantum on the Bay please."

"Sure thing Ms. Lady."

"So, driver, where are all the fun spots here in

Miami?"

"You must be new to the city."

"Yeah, I only been here a few months. I'm going to see this big-time photographer. I'm going to be a model."

The driver got really quiet. It was kind of weird because he had so much to say when I first got into the cab. As we drove down all the side streets I started to feel uneasy. He stopped at a stop sign and turned around looking at me funny.

"So, you're a model sweetie? How long have you been doing that?" he asked before pulling off.

"I've never modeled before. Do you run into a lot of girls who are models here?"

"Yeah, I see a lot of them, but I also see a lot of them running into the wrong people. Now I'm not telling you what to do, just be careful out here. Some of the guys in this city can be big creeps."

I didn't know if I should have taken him serious or just let it go. Here is a man that was in his forties telling me to be careful. I was a bit skeptical about him, but maybe he had a point. This is a new city for me, but I just had to test the waters. Collin and I were not seeing eye to eye and my money well was running dry.

Leaving behind Mario and Treyvon was a huge mistake and risk. I was not getting the money that I needed anymore so it was time to test the waters. My cab driver was pretty cute, but old. I leaned up in my seat and tapped his shoulder.

"So, I was thinking maybe after my meeting you could come back and get me? I mean if you're not too busy driving other girls around."

"I'll come back and get you and I will take you home. Don't get me wrong you're a very beautiful girl, but I have a wife and kids at home that I love and adore very much."

"Um, well ok. I was just wondering if you could show me around town. I don't have any friends here, and my fiancé and I are not on good terms." By the time he was about to answer we pulled up in front of this huge building.

"Where here. That will be twelve dollars."

"I should only be an hour; did you want me to call you when I'm done?"

"No, that won't be necessary. I will be out here waiting for you. Now if your not back in an hour you will have to call you another cab."

I gave him his money and I thanked him. As he pulled off I found myself standing in front of this amazing tall building. It was so many people going in and out, I had no clue who I was going to see. I texted Kenny and he told me to come up to the tenth floor. As I walked in I swear I felt like this was a dream. I had never been to a place like this.

Following everyone else to the elevators I went up to the tenth floor. The bubbles in my stomach were so loud everyone was looking at me funny. I hadn't eaten anything this morning, so my nerves were taking over. Hoping that this meeting go smoothly; I hadn't thought about what else I could be doing while I was in town. When I got off the elevator, it was a long line of girls waiting to be seen. I guess I wasn't the only one who wanted to be a model.

Standing in the line with all these other girls who were dressed in clothes that looked like they were painted on. Here I am with just some booty shorts on and a tank top; I thought I was overdressed. Still standing in the line I was hoping that I was seen before they left. From the looks of it I was the only good-looking girl too. These girls either looked like they were too young or too old. Some of the girls had missing teeth and smelled like they were drinking all night.

As the line got smaller and smaller the girls were coming out of the offices either mad as hell or crying. My nerves got even worse. Patiently waiting for my turn, only a few girls were happy coming out of the office. After waiting for over an hour it was finally my turn. As I walked in my heart dropped; as I saw a familiar face staring right back at me.

"Well aren't you just the prettiest thing that walked in here. What's your name pretty lady?"

Looking over at Camron I was afraid, nervous, and mad as hell that he was sitting right in front of me. Fidgeting with my fingers I made a smile appear on my face.

"Well, my name is Victoria and I'm here because I want to become a model. A guy named Kenny called me and asked me to show up." The three guys started laughing at me.

"Um, there is no Kenny that works with us, are you sure you are in the right place?"

"Yes," I said as I showed him the messages. "I was told to come here. I mean I can leave if you don't need me. I don't like my time being wasted. I have already stood in that long ass line of untalented, dirty, smelly looking ass women out there for you to tell me none of you texted me!" I yelled.

"Calm down little mama. You don't have to get all feisty. I'm Kenny. I only laughed because I didn't think the pictures you sent me were real. This is Camron, and this is Butch. We all run Dime-A-Dozen Modeling Agency."

As he was siting there fine as can be I couldn't help but to notice that Camron was sitting there staring at me. Just when I thought I was rid of him, here he is right back in my face. The last time we talked we had a really bad argument, and I was not about to let him get in the way of my money.

"Well am I hired or not?" I asked with an attitude, but with a smirk on my face.

"Yea, no doubt shorty your hired. We need someone like you on our team. Don't yall agree?" he asked his partners.

"Yeah, she will do just fine. Hell, she looks better than all the other hoes, I mean girls that walked up in here," Butch stated.

Licking his lips and undressing me with his eyes Camron spoke. "Yeah, she will do just fine. Seeing how she has a lot of mouth on her, she will fit in just right." Under his breath I heard him say "*I miss what that mouth do too.*"

"Excuse me, did you say something Camron?"

"Na, I ain't say nothing."

SECRETS OF AN UNFAITHFUL LOVER 2

"Well I want you to come back tomorrow around the same time, so we can get you started on your first job."

"Ok, cool and thanks so much for this opportunity," I said shaking their hands before walking out. I stood outside the door happy and jumping up and down. I could still hear them talking about me.

"Yo, shorty was on point, but she has a nasty attitude," Butch said.

"Aye, let me handle her. She just needs to be tamed," Camron responded.

I knew he was still into me and I was kind of glad that he was here. I missed him, and the money that he gave me. So maybe moving to Miami wasn't a bad idea. The fact that Collin no longer wants to be with me. I have to be prepared for what ever is about to happen. Going back down the elevator and out the door. I was hoping that my cabby was outside because I was ready to paint the town. I got some good news and I just wanted to enjoy the rest of my day. He was right where he said he would be.

"Hey, you came back for me."

"Yeah, I was just about to leave you. Did you get the job?"

"I did. I had an unexpected run in with someone from my past, but I guess everything is ok."

"Its's a guy isn't it?"

"How did you know? Is it written all over my face?"

"Your smile is way bigger now than it was this morning. I just hope that you are smart about this unexpected run-in. where am I taking you now Ms. Lady?"

"I need a nice drink to congratulate myself. Can you take me to the nearest bar, or where ever you think is best?"

"Sure, I know just a place. It's nice and laid back. I think you will really like it."

After a short ride we pulled up to a small little bar. It was not a lot of people sitting outside, and when I got out the car the cabby waved goodbye and pulled off. This time I didn't have to pay him; he was such a sweetheart. Having just a few drinks I called Collin to come get me, and might I say he was really pissed off.

When he picked me up he didn't even say a word to me. Not even when I told him that I landed a modeling job. He just drove us home and that was that. I spent the rest of my day in my room trying to figure out what to wear tomorrow. Money was back on my mind and nothing or nobody was going to get in the way of that. If Collin was going to be stingy with his money, then I will get it myself. My first job was to get back in good with Camron. I knew for a fact that he wouldn't mind throwing some cash my way. After all he miss this nice juicy wet pussy; I could tell it on his face when he saw me.

Chapter Five

Ж

This morning I woke up way before Collin did. I didn't want to ride around this beautiful city in a cab. So, after I took a quick shower I wrote Collin a letter and left. I didn't have time to hear his mouth nor tell me that he was taking the car. I had bigger plans for myself and I was not about to let him stop me from doing so. Leaving him behind I went back to Kenny's spot to see what they had planned.

The Miami sun was beaming down, and the air was pure. I was glad to be here. I made sure that I was dressed to impress. Waring an all pink skin-tight dress and some silver heels; I just knew I was sexy. Parking in the back lot, I noticed there were a few girls that were in the line from yesterday standing by the door talking.

"Girl did you see how sexy Camron was yesterday? I bet you he has a lot of girlfriends," One of them stated.

"I was paying attention to Kenny fine ass to even notice Camron. Hell, all three of them were acting thirsty as hell." The other girl said while laughing.

The third girl was just standing there laughing. As I walked up closer to them they all stared at me wondering who I was. I just walked past them and headed up to the tenth floor. I was anxious to see what they had in store for me. Even though Collin didn't approve; I was not going to let him get in the way of my money.

Waiting for the guys to come out and get me; the other girls made there way to sit down as well. I couldn't lie all three of them were gorgeous, but they seemed like they were very judgmental. Everybody that would walk past them they had something negative to say. I just sat there waiting nor more than a second later my phone was going off. As I looked down at my phone Collins name was peering across my screen. With hesitation I answered.

"Hello?"

"What the fuck Victoria! Why in the hell you just take my car? Then you leave a fucking note. You know I need my car to go find work!" he yelled.

"Well I needed it too Collin. It isn't like you can't take a cab like I have to. I am really busy right now; can I call you back?"

"Busy? Doing what?"

"I'm just busy. It's not like you care what I do seeing how you wont give me any money."

"Is that all you want me for is money? If you hadn't been cheating, then maybe I can trust you."

"I wasn't cheating Collin," I lied again. Every chance he got he was going to throw it up in my face.

"Victoria, I don't trust you. You have way too many secrets. Who's to say you're not being honest now?

"Well I need you to trust me right now. I landed a job yesterday; not like you care, but I think this will be good for me. I promise you everything will be fine."

"What ever Victoria. You still didn't have to take my fucking car!"

He hung up the phone. I could feel the fire from his voice still burning my ear as I put my phone back into my purse. When I got out the car the girls were staring at me; I just smiled. That's when one of them spoke to me.

"Hey, you're one of the new models?" she asked.

"Yeah, today is my first day. How long have yawl been modeling?"

"Well I have been doing this for over seven years, and they just started last week. Are you new to Miami?

"Yeah, I only been here for a couple of months. Kenny had me to come from Rio to be a model." I wasn't sure if it was something I said, or they just didn't like me.

All three girls were laughing again and whispering amongst themselves. "Is something wrong?"

"Na just didn't know Kenny was that desperate to get a girl all the way from Rio. So, what you speak Spanish or something?"

"yeah, I can speak a lot of different languages. Where are you from?" I asked. It was like she was grilling me. But before she could respond. Butch came out.

"Come on in ladies; Kenny is waiting," he said holding the door open for us.

"Well it's about damn time," the ring leader of the three musketeers said.

"Layla shut up and get your ass in here. Your always running your damn mouth and not doing enough work."

I laughed so hard to myself I know I was looking crazy. As we all went into the room; Kenny and Camron were waiting for us at the table. Collin kept calling my phone, so I just turned it off. I wasn't going to let him ruin anything for me. We all sat at the table as Kenny laid down his rules. He wanted each of us to talk to them separately. I didn't want anything to do with Camron, but from the looks of things I was stuck with him.

Camron was looking mighty tasty in his tight shirt with his dreads styled all neat. I couldn't help but to stare at his chest and his lips as he talked to me about what the company was about and my job. I was not focusing on any rules he said or none of the business plans that they had, I was just thinking about him.

Collin and I hadn't had sex the whole time we been here, and I was dying to get this little itch that I had scratched. As he continued to talk I placed my hand on his lap. Slowly sliding my hand towards the middle of his thigh. I just had to see if he was feeling the same way I was. As my hand gotten closer to his penis I felt his pants jump. I began to smile, whispered in his ear.

"You know I missed kissing all over your sexy body."

"Aren't you married? Kenny told me you was here with your dude," he replied moving my hand off his thigh.

"Don't act like that, you know you still want me."

"That might be true, but I don't want to get in the way of what yawl got going on. Lets just get back to business. Now you will be doing a lot of photo shoots, private parties, and video shoots. We will pay for all your trips, hotel fees, and everything else. Now do you think that you can handle all of that? I mean without your husband getting in the way?"

"First of all, he's not my husband. We haven't had sex in a long time. So, I can care less how he feels about what I'm doing. Do you live close?" I wasn't worried about all that other shit he was talking. My pussy was throbbing and wet, and I needed him to fix it like he always did. "Can you show me where the bathroom is?" I asked looking up at everybody else.

"Man come on. We have a lot of work to do and your bull-shittin'."

"Don't act like you don't want to be near me. You know I can make you smile more ways than one."

"Yeah and you also got me fired too. I don't know what you said to your friends, but you are the reason I even moved to the states," he complained.

"I didn't tell anybody anything. Why would I do that knowing I could have been kicked out of school? Maybe it was one of the other girls you was fucking, but it wasn't me."

"It don't even matter. What did you want to talk to me about anyway?"

"Well now that I have you by myself, I'll show you what I wanted."

Camron was standing by the mans bathroom. I pushed him inside and locked the door behind him. I wasn't taking no for an answer. I couldn't help myself. He was just calling my name with his fine ass body. I knew if I teased him some more he would give into me. As I took off my shirt my breast were staring at him. I didn't have a bra on, so he had easy access. Grabbing his hands, I placed them on my beast and from there the fire started. He couldn't resist me.

Not worried about anybody walking in he pulled me closer to him. kissing me with passion I knew he missed me more than he led on. His penis went from limp to rock solid in a matter of seconds. Unzipping his pants, I slid my hand down to caress his nice long penis. His eyes was rolling in the back of his head as I was stroking him. I couldn't just let his erection go to waist, so I slid my shorts down and slid his penis inside me. It was easy for him to slide inside because I didn't have any panties on either. I knew what I wanted, and I got just that. It was feeling so good he began to get loud.

"Fuck Victoria! You know I couldn't resist yo' fine ass," he said holding onto my breast.

"I knew you couldn't resist me daddy, you were just playing hard to get in front of your friends."

"This shit always wet as hell. You knew exactly what you were doing." He began to go faster and faster. I got louder. I knew somebody heard us. "Yea baby, back that ass up. FUCK!" he yelled.

I felt amazing. Not only was I working I was getting what I needed. Sex was what I craved. He was hitting every wall and spot I had. I swear he was swimming in my juices. I could have sex with him every day if I could. After ten minutes there was a knock at the door.

"Aye Cam, you in there?"

"Yeah bro, I'll be out in a minute." He continued to stroke himself inside of me. "My stomach hurt; it must be something I ate," Camron replied. We both started laughing.

"Have you seen Victoria? She hasn't come back yet?" he asked still standing by the bathroom door.

"Yeah, she went to my car to get my wallet. Ill go get her; here I come."

"Ahight bro, hurry up. We got a lot of work to do."

As we listened for Kenny to walk away we finished up. He was going even faster until he came on my lower back.

"OH SHIT!" he yelled. I had to cover up his mouth he was so loud.

"Damn boo that was a big one. When was the last time you had any pussy?" I asked walking to the sink to clean myself off.

"It's been a while. I'm glad that you're here now, maybe I don't have to wait that long for the next time," he laughed.

"Yeah, well as long as you don't change on me, then we shouldn't have any problems."

"What do you mean by that?"

"You know I'm with Collin. Our relationship is strictly business with occasional sex," I said peeking out the door. He was still cleaning himself up and fixing his clothes.

"You know me, I will take what I can get. Who can pass up your sexy ass. You just do something to me when I'm near you."

He was steady talking while I was trying to make sure the cost was clear. I had to sneak out of this bathroom, but he couldn't keep his hands off my ass. I didn't see anyone in the hallway, so I walked out. Camron coming out right behind me; we both walked in the room. All of them were staring at us like they seen a ghost. Kenny had a huge smirk on his face, and a he walked towards Camron they gave each other a hand shake. I just shook my head and sat down.

I could feel the tension in the room from the girls. They were staring at me like they wanted to say something. I know they were mad at me for whatever reason they had, but I didn't give a fuck. I had to make my money, and if that meant I had to fuck Camron to ensure that; then that what I was going to do. Kenny sat down next to what's her face and he started talking.

"Now that we are all back in one room, I have some jobs for you girls. Kianna, you are in charge of the clothes that yawl will ware." She had a pissed look on her face, I guess she wanted something better to do. "Layla, you are in charge of making sure we all eat, now that is going to be easy seeing how yawl have to watch what yawl eat. Victoria, you will be in charge of making sure each girl is here on time. I want you to keep tabs on them too." Kianna's face went sour. "We will take care of the rest. Now I don't want any bull shit, nor anybody to be late or you will get a pay cut."

"Speaking of pay, how much is we making?" Kianna asked. Grabbing the envelops sitting in front of him, he passed them around. "What the hell are these?"

"Just open the damn envelope," Kenny said with frustration.

We all opened up our envelopes. The other girl that was sitting next to Layla didn't get one. She was just sitting there all quiet not saying a word. Butch walked over to her and asked her to follow him. They headed out the door, but when Butch came back, she wasn't with him. We all was looking around the room in silence. We all got back to work planning our very first event. As we was all just sitting there I took a glance at my phone and noticed that it was getting late. I knew that Collin was going to be really pissed off at me.

I left around 8:30pm. Camron was trying to get me to go home with him to finish what we started, but I told him he had to wait. As much as I wanted to fuck him again; I still had Collins car. Pulling up to the house a quarter after nine, Collin was sitting outside on the porch. As I was getting out the car he walked up to me yelling.

"Really Victoria!"

"What is it now Collin?"

"So, you're just going to act like you haven't been gone all day? You must think I'm stupid."

"Collin I'm tired. I have had a long day. All you want to do is argue."

"Hell yeah, I want to argue! You take my car and don't answer my fucking phone calls. I don't know what got into you but, you need to get your shit together or I'm moving back to Rio," Collin said walking into the house after me.

"Man, Collin you buggin'. Damn all I wanted to do was make some money for myself and you always try to find a way to get in the middle of that. Você não vai me dar nenhum dinheiro. Eu juro que você age como seu meu pai, ele está morto Lembre-se. Isso é tão jogado fora. Tudo o que você quer fazer é discutir, não me foder, nem ter certeza de que estou feliz," I said going up the stairs to take a shower.

"Don't you walk away from me, speak to me in English. We are far away from Rio. I swear your acting like a spoiled bitch," he yelled. "Now all of a sudden you want to take a shower at night. You always took one in the morning. What you do get some dick today instead of working?"

"You know what Collin I don't like your attitude. And if I did get some dick at least they want to fuck me. You on the other had wont. Why Collin? Are you creeping around?"

"You know damn well I'm not the one who has cheated. Look you better get your shit together for real, because I am really at the end of my wits with you and your games. We have been engaged for far too long."

Taking my clothes off I noticed that Camron's number fell out my shorts pocket. I was hoping that Collin didn't notice. He was getting on my last nerve. I promised him if he did right I would do right, but he just nagged way too much. Going into the bathroom, I noticed that Collin was watching my every move.

"So, what did you do today Victoria, you want me to take a shower with you?"

"Na, I'm good. Don't want to take a shower with me now. You wasn't just screaming that before. Now can you close the door please."

Collin slammed the door behind him. I know I pissed him off even more, but I had other things on my brain. Camron had my pussy still throbbing and wet. Letting the steaming hot water hit my aroused body; I played with my sensitive clit. I knew I had another orgasm left in me, so I played with myself until I came. I know I was loud, but I didn't care. Collin wasn't doing his job, so I had to make do. After I got done with my shower, when I turned the water off I heard the front door slam. I dried myself off and climbed into our king size bed. I text

Camron I nice message. "I can't wait to kiss on your sexy body again," I said adding kissy face emojis and the eggplant emoji. As I waited on his response I dozed off with my hands tucked between my legs thinking about my next meeting with my boo Camron. I was going to make every meeting count.

<u>Chapter Six</u>

Ж

A couple of months had past, and Collin and I still wasn't seeing eye to eye. Last week he made a phone call to his parents and I overheard him telling them that he was homesick. I knew sooner or later he was going to want to move back home, but I dint know it was this soon. Collin had landed a job at a high-end retail store that he also models for. I never understood how he could be upset at me for being a model when he is too. We only been here a short time and we argue more than before.

Waking up horny, I rolled over to see if Collin was still sleep. He was moving in his sleep, so I just climbed on top of him. He was trying to push me off, but I began kissing him on his neck. He laid there for a bit before he tossed my ass back on my side of the bed.

"Look I'm moving back home with my parents next week. I can't keep doing this with you," he said putting on his pajama pants.

It was early Saturday morning, so neither one of us had shit to do. I was just trying to put the spice back into our relationship. I definitely was trying to avoid him wanting to move back home. I did what any desperate woman would do, beg. Hell, I needed him to stay. At the end of the day he was taking care of me.

"Baby I'm sorry please don't leave me. You know I don't have anybody. My parents are dead, and I still don't have a real job. What will I do without you?" I begged.

"Don't try and act like you want me here. You promised me one too many times that you were faithful. Tell me really, how many guys you have slept with?"

I looked at him then at my phone. Was he really going to keep asking me about the same thing over and over. What did he want me to say that I slept with five different men? I was not about to put myself in a even worse position. Knowing that I had to keep him happy I lied yet again.

"Collin, I haven't had sex with anybody. Now I know you don't believe me."

"Damn right I don't," he said with his arms folded.

"I haven't slept with anybody. Now will you please just stay so we can work this out?" I was hoping that I could persuade his mind, but from the looks of it he was still not listening to me.

"Victoria, I really don't have time for this. It's a Saturday morning and I just spent the last hour talking to you in circles. Now I love you, but this is beyond wrong. You know things haven't been right for a long time."

Collin walked away without saying a word. When I followed behind him he made it up to the room and shut the door. I went back down stairs and started to make some breakfast. I whipped up some eggs, bacon, toast and some grits with cheese. I knew he couldn't turn down my food. I know that I'm a handful, but he always fell like he was in control of my life. Walking his food back up to him, the tv was really loud. He was watching a movie.

"Here love I made you some breakfast."

"What you put in it, poison?"

"No," I laughed holding his plate. "Why would you think I would do something like that?"

"Because I know your mad at me, so you could have anything up your sleeves."

"Come on now baby, I wouldn't do that to you. I just wanted to show you how much I love you," I said trying to butter him up. I was getting annoyed with all the back and forth. I just had to keep the peace between us, so he wouldn't leave.

"What are you up to Victoria?" I thought of something quick.

"I think it's time for us to get married Collin. We have been together for a long time. I love you and I only want to be with you." He looked at me in demise. I had to say something that would change his mind and fast.

"Wait what?" he said putting a fork full of food in his mouth. "You really want to get married Victoria?"

"I mean yeah why not. I was thinking maybe we can just elope, why have a big wedding when it can just be me and you." He looked at me with a sexy glare. I wasn't sure what he was thinking, but he put his plate down and headed towards me.

"So, your telling me that you are ready to settle down and have children?" he asked grabbing my hand with a huge grin on his face. I wasn't saying all that, but I had to make it believable for him to want to stay.

"Well we can, just not right now. You know I want to see how my career goes as a model."

"Model?" he questioned me. "I thought that was a joke. You are really trying to be a model?"

What kind of question was that, am I trying to be a model. I swear he knew just how to piss me off. Next thing I knew I pulled away from him with my arms crossed. His phone started to ring and so did mine. He went down stairs and I laid down on my bed. Looking at who was calling my whole vibe got better. It was Camron.

"Hello," I answered with a sexy voice.

"What chu doing beautiful?"

"Nothing just got into a little argument with Collin," I told him.

"Awe sorry to hear that. What are you doing today? Maybe I can take you out on the town."

SECRETS OF AN UNFAITHFUL LOVER 2

"Oh really? That would be fun." As soon as I
agreed Collin walked in.

"What would be great," he asked holding his phone
to his ear.

"Some of the girls from the agency wants to show
me around town," I lied. "Do you mind if I go?"

"You have to ask your man's permission to leave?"
Camron asked.

"No, he just walked in being nosey. What time you
want to come get me. He's acting funny with his car."

"Send me your location I'm coming to get you now,
so get dressed," he said before hanging up and waiting on
my answer.

*"What the hell am I going to tell Collin if he see's
Camron pull up?"* I asked myself. I paced back and forth
thinking of something that he would believe. He was
already on edge, so one false move would have him

93

tripping again. "Collin eu vou estar indo para o sore em breve, você quer que eu te trazer alguma coisa de volta bebê?"

"Sim, preciso de algumas coisas para o jantar. Estava pensando em comida do mar. Pegue algumas cervejas também, Oh e um pouco de deserto. Pegue uma nota de cem dólares da minha cômoda," he said back.

Going back into the room I did what he said. I took the money out of his money clip. Even though I didn't really feel like going to the store. I just wanted to spend time will Camron. He wanted my attention, so I was going to give it to him. Texting Camron telling him where to meet me I left the house. Collin was sitting on the couch talking to his mom on the phone. I walked down four to five houses from ours before Camron pulled up beside me.

"Where the hell are you going shorty?" he asked laughing.

"Waiting on you. I didn't want him seeing me get into your car."

"Well you need to leave him then. You can't be happy with him, I can tell."

"How can you tell?"

"If you was then you wouldn't be sitting next to me, so I ask why are you with him?" I thought about that question every day.

"I guess I do love him. we have been together for a very long time. I guess I just wish he would just give me what I need sexually. Everything else he does is fine."

"So, he's not cleaning your pipes out?"

"Camron shut up!" I said laughing. "That's what I have you for right?"

"So, am I the only one?" I looked at him and grabbed his dick in my hand.

"Yeah, for the time being," I replied laughing.

"Don't play with me. Your not in college anymore. I mean I don't care who you fuck, just know I better not catch anything."

"Shut up, Where are we going anyway?" I asked looking out the window. The way he was going; I never been before. The houses were a lot bigger and nicer. "So, do you live over here?"

"Yeah, play your cards right then maybe you can have one of your own."

"So, you're going to let me live with you?" I said as a joke.

"Naw, your married remember. So, unless you planning on leaving him for me, then you are in a fucked-up situation. I know you can't get enough of this big dick, so I'm willing to give you some for now."

"For now?" I asked. "Damn you're trying to get rid of me that quick?"

"Na, I was just fucking with you. So, what do you think about the other girls?"

"Your talking about the ones I model with?"

"Yeah, are you cool with them?"

"Yeah, we tight as hell," I said laughing. "Na but I don't talk to them. The girl Layla like you, don't she?"

"Why you say that?"

"Oh nothing."

We drove for another ten minutes then we stopped at this really nice big house. The outside was painted white with some red shutters, kind of like the nice houses you see on the movies. The houses next door had gates, and some didn't. when we got out I heard dogs barking.

"How are you liking it here so far?" he asked as he was walking up to his front door.

"I love it here, oh my God this place is amazing. I was shocked to know that you were here too."

"Yeah, this is where I'm shorty, I thought I told you."

"Um, noo. So why were you all the way in Rio?" I asked being nosey. A fine man like him should have been here with a wife and kids stashed somewhere.

"I was there for a job intern in college and ended up staying. I'm glad I did too; or I wouldn't have met your sexy ass."

I started blushing. He opened the door and my mouth dropped. His house was amazing inside. He has chandeliers dangling from the ceiling, and, the floors were amazing. I felt like I was in a movie. Everything that a woman could ever want and need. There was animal fur on the floor and expensive paintings on the walls. In the back of my mind I was picturing myself living with him and making a life with him. Collin would've thought this was too much. A woman like me needs to be living lavish, but I guess I just have to fake it and keep this love affair going. As soon as I began to get comfortable; Collin called me. I hesitated to answer.

"Hello," I said trying to whisper.

"Where are you babe?"

"I'm still at the store, what's up do you need anything?"

"Damn, how long are you going to be? You know it don't take that long to get a few things. I'm hungry."

"Really Collin, I'll be home soon."

"Why the hell are you whispering? Where are you at for real Victoria?"

"por favor, não comece comigo, Collin. Nós temos feito o bem. Estou na loja. Eu estarei em casa logo Ok!"

"Não tenha atitude. Só volte para casa, por favor. Este lugar não é como um bebê em casa. Não quero que te aconteça nada," he replied.

"Ok meu amor eu vou estar em casa em breve."

Hanging up the phone, I followed Camron to the other room. Still amazed at how well he kept his home, I ignored the fact that I just told Collin I was on my way home. I was not ready to leave. I had to see the rest of his home before I left.

"So, do you live alone?" I asked being nosey.

"Yeah, it's just me. So, your dude wants you to come home huh?" I looked at him with a shocking look on my face.

"What makes you say that?" I asked smiling from ear to ear.

"I'll take you home, so you wont get into any trouble," he said laughing.

"I'm not ready to go home yet."

Walking up to him I placed my hands on his chest. I was getting what I came for. Even though I told Collin I was on my way home, I was not about to let this sexy man out my sight. As I began to kiss him; he picked me up into his arms. His strong arms held me against his muscular body. The smell of his cologne lingered seeping into my nose. Feeling the sexual attraction between us was intense.

I knew that he wanted me just as much as I wanted him. right in the middle of our fourplay; Collin called again. So, I just went ahead and left. Camron dropped me off at the store and I could tell he was pissed off at me. Telling him bye; he just drove off without saying a word. That man just did something to me. He knew how to make my panties wet, and my nipples hard. I just had to have him inside me again one way or another.

Walking around the store that I never been in was horrible. I didn't know where anything was; and I swear I felt dumb. Thinking about Camron I damn near forgot all the things that Collin asked for. After an half an hour of shopping I was finally on my way back to the house.

Coming in the house with the food Collin requested, I cooked and went to bed. My hormones were so high that I just played with myself and went to bed; not even caring what and or how Collin felt.

<u>Chapter Seven</u>

Ж

A couple of months had passed, and I managed to get Collin to stay. After being at his job for a while, the money was getting too good to him. I kept telling him going back to Rio was a bad idea, so I guess now he understands. We still haven't set a date yet for the wedding, but I'm really worried. I have still been doing me.

Camron and I have been seeing one another a lot lately. We have been meeting up after photo shoots and parties that they host. Honestly, I think it's getting pretty serious between us. I know that it's wrong, but I can tell that Layla is felling some type of way too. Every time she see's me she has something smart to say. I guess she feels threatened. But I didn't see why when she was fucking Kenny.

Today we had to go to this major event where a lot of important people would be there. I was excited too.

Maybe this would be my big break and become a model for a major company. Don't get me wrong, Camron and his crew were great, but they weren't giving me all that I needed. Camron told me to meet him at the Biltmore Hotel. I wasn't exactly sure where that was, but it sounded like a nice place to be.

Collin was already gone; it was about three in the afternoon. I had to be at the hotel around five. I called a cab and was on my way. This time I had a different driver. I still wasn't all the way familiar with Miami, but I was getting the feel of the roads to take. We passed so many places that I wanted to visit like clothing store, hair salons, and this little boutique that had vintage clothes. So that Collin wouldn't be worried, I text and told him that I wouldn't be home. I didn't get a response. When I pulled up Kenny and Layla was standing outside.

"Hey, where's Camron?" I asked getting out the cab. They started laughing.

"Awe your man ain't here yet," Kenny said grabbing onto Layla's waist.

"What's so funny?" I asked Layla since she kept laughing.

"Nothing girl, are you ready for this shoot?"

"Yeah, who all coming?"

"Just a few big-time rappers, and some other models. So that means ya'll need to be on ya'll a game. I will not book shit else if ya'll fuck up."

Walking into the hotel it was swarming with other girls. Camron was still not here. I was starting to get worried. Why would he ask me to come if he wasn't going to be here? I didn't trust Kenny nor his sneaky ass bitch. Not paying them any attention I went to the bathroom to fix my face. I was walking passed some ugly ass women as well as some beautiful women. I couldn't help but be jealous, so I knew I had to bring the heat. As soon as I made it to the women's bathroom door I heard a soft voice speak.

"Hey, are you going to be modeling with us today?" When I turned my head, it was this beautiful super model by the name of Jazmine staring at me.

"Yeah, I'm so nervous," I said turning around to talk to her. "How do you get over your nerves?"

"Girl don't sweat it. You will do just fine. I normally just take a pill, or I have a few drinks before I go on stage. It's always a guy out there that won't leave you alone."

"Fa real? See I don't have time for no thirsty ass dude bothering me. Are we working here?"

"Yeah, they have a big ballroom upstairs. Who are you here with?" I wasn't sure why she was being so nice to me, but it was a breath of fresh air.

"I was supposed to meet my agent Camron, but he's nowhere to be found. Who are you here with?"

"Starlite Modeling Agency. We are always looking for new faces if you want to join our team."

"That's a really good idea," I replied. She gave me her number and a cup of patron. I was beyond nervous.

We both went into the bathroom to get dressed and headed upstairs. It was time for us to all perform, but Camron was still not in site. I don't know what he was trying to prove, but I was getting really upset. I text him again to dee what he was doing.

"Hey babe, where are you?"

"Brah, I'm at the hotel, where you at?"

"I'm upstairs, I was down there waiting on you since I got here. I'm so nervous. I need to see you before I perform."

"Ahight boo, here I come. Do you have on that black lace I bought you?"

"Yeah, I'm by the elevators on the tenth floor. I'm with Jazmine."

"Jazmine who?"

"The super model. She was very nice to me when I came in, so I just stayed with her."

"The real skinny Jazmine with the big ass titties."

"Yeah, why do you know her," I asked with concern.

"Yeah, I know her. Here I come. Just go in I'll be up there in a minute."

I wasn't sure what all that was about, but I went into the room and sat all the way in the back to wait for Camron. Jazmine was still standing in the hallway. I waited for about ten minutes and still no Camron. I went back out to the hallway to see if he was coming out the elevator, but instead he was talking to Jazmine. I went right up to them both to see what was going on.

"Hey babe," I said latching my arm to his.

"What's good Victoria. Give me a second." He said pushing me off of him.

"Awe is that your little toy now?" she said laughing.

"Na, she's one of my models like you use to be. How you been though?" he asked her.

I stood right next to them as they talked. I felt really weird listening to them. Even though Camron and I wasn't official I still didn't like the fact he was entertaining her in front of me. So, I went back over to them and interrupted.

"Well it's time for us to go in boo, are you ready?"

"I'll be ready when I'm finished. Now you go in and get yourself ready. This has nothing to do with you," he said shooing off.

As I walked away he grabbed Jazmine's arm and walked the opposite direction. The evet was about to start so I just went in and showed my ass. It was a lot of music artist and other modeling agencies there. Each girl had to walk across the stage a few times, then we had to mingle. I was way too nervous. I didn't know exactly how to talk to these guys. They were all staring at me like a piece of meat.

We had to dance for them. I didn't know this was apart of the job description. I just wanted to model. Jazmine was doing it all from drinking to snorting, and everything else that they had her do. She was making money though and that's what I came here for. So, I walked over to one of the tables where a bunch of rappers were and did what I had to do.

Camron was still paying a whole lot of attention to Jazmine. I just went and did my thing. Making sure that I went home with a lot of money I drank more, and I even tried some crack. Sniffing it into my nose; the burning sensation was not a good feeling.

After my second dose I was feeling funny, but it made me come out of my shell. I danced with so many people that I didn't even know. That's when I started to feel really bad. My head was spinning, and I couldn't keep myself up. That's when a familiar voice walked over to me.

"Come with me sweetie. I will get you comfortable," the woman said guiding me.

"Where are we going?"

"I'm taking you to my room so that you can get some rest." It sounded like Jazmine, but I wasn't sure. I didn't want to really talk to her because she was all in Camron's face.

"I need to get home; what time is it?"

"It's a little after ten, you can stay here with me tonight if you like," she said getting me through her door. I couldn't go home like this, but if I didn't go home I would have serious problems.

"I just need to sleep this off," I said. "Then I will catch a cab home."

"Ok, well I will lay with you just in case. Don't worry I wont let anything happen to you."

Even though I wasn't at all to fond of Jazmine; she was the only one who came to my rescue. Camron's no-good ass still didn't come in and check on me. I closed my eyes and went to sleep. I needed to make sure Collin didn't find out anything that I was doing.

Chapter Eight

Ж

"Oh my God, my head is killing me," I said lifting my body off the bed I was laying on. After lifting up I looked around to see if I saw Collin, but he wasn't there.

"Good morning beautiful." I instantly popped up worried and confused.

"Oh my God! Why didn't you wake me up? I was supposed to go home last night!" I yelled reaching for my phone.

"Yeah you had a lot of missed calls and messages, so I just turned your phone off and let you sleep," Jazmine said.

"I have to go, I need a ride home. Can you please take me home?"

"Sure hun. I have a meeting soon anyway. How far do you live?"

"Just a few blocks away. Where did Camron go? Is he still here?"

"Na, he left last night. I'm so sorry; I just thought you needed some rest."

Turning on my phone it started going off like crazy. Collin had called me over thirty times and texted me. I knew that once I got home; he was going to go off. I had never stayed gone over night since we moved here. Gathering my things Jazmine and I left the hotel. On top of that Camron left me hanging too. I was so sure he would at least made sure I was ok or got home safe. After all I came here because of him. I was pissed and texted him to let him know how I felt, but he didn't respond.

"So how did you like the party?" Jazmine asked as we were walking to her car.

"It was very different. I didn't know it was going to be like that? Are all the parties like that?"

"Girl, yes. In this industry you have to be ready to do anything to secure that money bag. How long you and Camron been dating?"

"Oh, we're not dating. He's just my manager." I lied.

"Yeah, he used to be mines too. That was until he wanted to be more. You watch out for him he's a real ass."

"Yeah?"

"Yea. Girl he tried to get me to do a movie with him and his friends. As soon as I turned him down he dropped me from my contract."

Taking in everything she said I was surely concerned about Camron. But the whole time we were dealing with one another he never acted funny. I told her where I stayed, and we was on our way. She lived not that far from where I was, so it was pretty cool. I guess I know had my very first friend in Miami, and she was a bad ass beautiful model.

Walking into the house I noticed that it was quiet; a little bit too quiet. Calling out for Collin he didn't answer. I ran up the stairs to see if he was in the room, but he wasn't. I called out for him once more but there was still no reply. I was hoping that he was just in the kitchen ignoring me, but he wasn't in there either. I called his phone and waited for him to answer.

"Hello," he answered with anger in his voice.

"Baby where are you?" I asked. I knew he was pissed off, but it wasn't my fault this time. "Baby, say something," I said listening to him breath.

"What's the point of trying with you Victoria if you wont do right by me?"

"Collin I can explain. I was at a modeling job, and I drank too much and fell asleep."

"Fell asleep Victoria? Who do you think I am. And what the hell were you doing drinking? You don't fucking drink. What kind of people are you around?"

"Collin I was working, making money for us. I'm sorry. It wont happen again. Besides my new friend Jazmine mad sure I was ok and got me home safe."

"I guess. I will be home a little later. Maybe you need to chill in the house for a bit. I don't want you getting caught up in anything you or I can't handle."

"Ok Collin."

After hanging up the phone I texted Camron again to have him call me immediately. I just couldn't believe that he did me like that. Not only was he ignoring me last night, he left me there drunk and with people I didn't know. After an half an hour he had finally called me.

"Hey, you," I said answering the phone."

"What do you want Victoria?" looking down at my phone. I was shocked at what I was hearing.

"What's your problem?"

"Nothing, I'm busy. What do you want?"

"So that's where were at now? Do you remember that last time you tried to dismiss me?"

"Come on man damn, I'm working. You always have to be in fucking charge. I will come get you later on ok?"

"What if I don't want to go Camron?"

"Well I don't know what to tell you. We have another job tonight. So, either be ready by seven or you can look for you another job."

He hung up on me and I was just standing there looking dumb. Collin had just told me to stay in the house, but I needed to keep making money. Last night I made over two thousand dollars. Even though I was not being myself, it felt good doing something I wanted to do. I went and took a shower to get the alcohol off my skin, and I ate some breakfast. I was going back and forth in my head what I wanted to do. A couple of hours had past and Collin still wasn't home. I had gotten bored, so I called Jazmine to see if she was going to be working tonight. The phone rang a few times before she answered.

"Hello?"

"Hey girl. What you doing today?"

"Girl, I have this photo shoot to do with this new model tonight. Do you want to come with me?"

"Yeah, id rather come chill with you then to get aggravated by Camron tonight. He still has an attitude."

"Well girl I will be to get you in about an hour. Dress to impress. You never know who's going to show up tonight."

"Ok girl, I will text you when I'm ready."

Since I had already taken my shower I picked out the perfect outfit. Pink under lace shirt with a skin-tight black skirt suit. Made sure my legs were shaved as well as my bikini line. Even though I had already cleaned myself up the night before; you could never be to cautious. Collin still hadn't made it home yet, so when Jazmine pulled up I just left.

"Hey girl," I said opening up her passenger door."

"Girl I swear these modeling agencies always have me so busy. I will be leaving to go to New York in a couple of weeks. Your more than welcome to come with if you want." I looked at her with a smile on my face. She was the only one who was being nice to me since I've been here.

"Ok girl, I sure will go with you. I have never been anywhere else. I can't wait to travel."

It took us about twenty minutes to get to our destination. We pulled up to this big house that had about thirty or more cars parked out front. As I began to look at each one; I saw one that looked pretty familiar.

"Do you know who's house were at?"

"No who?"

"Willi Shabez."

"Who's he," I asked. I wasn't familiar with anyone that big yet.

"He's a major movies producer. He books models to be extras. I have to do a shoot for him with this new model named Cannon or something like that."

I knew that Collin was a model for his job, and the car we rode past looked just like his. Helping her with her things after we parked, I was sure that Collin was the guy she was talking about. How an he tell me not to work and he's out here modeling with pretty girls and not even tell me.

We had to have walked up thirty stairs. I couldn't even count how many windows it had. I could jut imagine how many bedrooms and bathrooms it had. Seeing places like this just made me want to work harder and get more money. Being a girl from Rio I've always had what I wanted. Now that my parents are dead and gone I have to get things myself. Collin only gives me what he thinks I need.

Walking in behind other people as they greeted the man standing at the door. When we go to him I felt chills come over my body. He was the finest man that I have since we have been here. He shook my hand really tight and gave a smile that will have you weak to your knees.

"Who was that," I asked Jazmine still looking behind me at him.

"That was Willi," she said.

"That was Willi?" I replied in shock.

"Girl yes. Ain't he a tall drink of water?"

"Girl he a tall glass of wine. I can't wait to get to know him."

"Well girl get in line. Every girl wants him, and every guy wants to be him. I have to go get dressed, so find a nice seat and enjoy the show."

Still amazed at what I was seeing I found a nice seat in the middle of the room. Everyone else were still coming in taking there seats. Some of them were couples and they were just talking away enjoying each-others company. I started to think about Camron, Collin wouldn't have wanted to come to something like this. I texted Camron and told him where I was and the text I got back was nothing short of sweet. He had the nastiest attitude ever. So, I just stopped texting him, and turned off my phone.

Sitting there waiting on the show to start; a lot more people began to take their seats. The walls surrounding me were filled with pictures, paintings, and expensive art work. The more I looked around the more I wanted to stay. I wanted to enjoy this house with William. Even if it was for just one night; I wanted to enjoy sleeping in such a beautiful home.

As everyone took their seats they started clapping. When I looked up there he was. Mr. William himself standing with grace. His clean cut all white suit and his all white shoes. He started to speak thanking everyone for attending his event. He said something about a new clothing line he had. I was so stuck on him talking that I didn't notice that he had stopped, and the models began to come out. They were all dressed in white, and they looked beautiful.

They began to walk pass me and right next to Jazmine was a surprising face. Collin was the guy that she was talking about. He didn't tell me he knew her, nor that

he had a major job tonight. He kept trying to get me to stay

home. When he saw me, his face went pale. Maybe Collin

too had skeletons in his closet, and I was going to find out

one way or another.

Chapter Nine: The After-Party

Ж

After all of the models were finished they scattered into the crowed to mingle. I tried my best to get over that fact that Collin was here, and he didn't tell me. A lot of the older people that attended left. Now it was all of the younger crowd. Jazmine was mingling with people, so I decided to get up and do the same.

Walking around I noticed how everyone was comfortable talking to each other and laughing. Willi was also talking to everyone thanking them for coming. I went over to the open bar and grabbed me a dink. There were so many choices I didn't know what to get, so I just grabbed a glass of white wine. I didn't want to get too drunk like I did last night. As I was standing there I felt a tap on shoulder. It scared the shit out of me that I spilled my wine.

"I'm so sorry," the male voice said grabbing a napkin to help me clean off my skirt.

"It's ok. It was an accident," I replied turning towards him. When I fully faced him; I was stunned. It was Mr. Willi himself. "Mr. Santiago I'm so sorry. Did I get any on you?"

"No, looks like I got it all on you. I apologize for startling you." I was so nervous. Out of all the beautiful women in here he chose to talk to me. "Other than the spilled drink are you having a good time?"

"Yes, I really like how you set up your home. I have never seen a place this beautiful. Do you always have things like this here?" I asked still cleaning myself off.

"Yeah, I try to host a lot of events. Do you want to go somewhere a lot quieter, so we can talk?"

"Sure," I replied. He latched his arm with mine and we walked away from the bar. "How long have you been in the business?"

"Which business," he said laughing. I felt like I had put my foot in my mouth. I knew nothing about this man, but yet he was interested in talking to me. "My name is planted in a lot of things. I try to add more, but always staying within my fields. Are you a model?"

"Yeah, how did you know," I said blushing again.

"Your too beautiful to be anything else."

"*Not he flirting with me!*" I said to myself. We walked up his long stairwell. He had so many rooms up here, and lots more expensive pictures. I was shocked and amazed. Leaving everyone alone downstairs it was so quiet up here. He was showing me some of the famous people he met, or liked like Michel Jackson, Jessie Baker, Elvis Presley, and more. I began to picture myself knowing them too.

"Wow, you know a lot of people. You must really like your job."

"Yeah, it pays the bills. It's not what you know it's who you know."

As we were talking Collin texted me asking where I was. I ignored him because I was networking. I wanted to get to know him more, not just because he was taking interest in me, but because maybe just maybe I could connect with his friends and get more money. All in all, this a party filled with potential clients. I was a model, and I was looking for a better paying job.

Ever since I had been working for Camron I only had made a few thousand bucks, but it wasn't enough. I had to figure out a way to get him to have me on his team, so I did what I needed to do.

"So, do you have any room for little ole me in your busy schedule?" I asked rubbing up against him pushing him to the wall.

"Well, we always have room for new and beautiful faces," he replied rubbing on my face. I gave off a little chuckle retracing the direction of his hand. "When can you star…?"

"Immediately!" I said with excitement. "I mean immediately," I repeated holding back my composure.

"Give me a call tomorrow and we will work out the details. I have a very special job for you."

We had made it to the other side of his stairway. Holding on to his arm, I was grinning from ear to ear. I was enjoying everything that he was talking about. He made me laugh and he kept telling me how beautiful I was. When we made it to the bottom of the stairs I noticed Collin walking in our direction.

"It was so nice talking to you, but I have to go. I will definitely give you a call tomorrow," I said trying not to be even more obvious. Collin was getting closer.

"Ok beautiful I will be waiting on you," he said as he kissed my had. By the time he let my hand go Collin was right behind me and William was walking away.

"What are you doing here!" he questioned me.

"My friend Jazmine invited me. We had a show together yesterday remember. I told you she brought me home this morning."

"Yeah, I guess. Why were you talking to Mr. Santiago?"

"Oh, he was just tanking me for coming that's all. Are you ready to go home now? You did a really good job tonight babe," I said to take the heat off of me.

"Thanks, Jazmine set everything up for me."

He grabbed my hand and we headed for the door. I was so happy that he didn't push the issue of me being here. How I looked at it he couldn't be mad for me being here because he didn't even tell me he was coming. We left and headed home. The whole ride home was quiet. I couldn't tell if he was upset or he was really believing what I had told him. Looking out the window I was thinking about Mr. Santiago; Camron was in the far back of my mind. I just found me a new money machine, and I was going to get as much coins in my purse as I needed. No matter who it hurt in the end I was doing what was best for me.

Chapter Ten: Flashback /Age Fifteen

Ж

Waking up to the alluring smell of breakfast cooking. I knew my mom was going her thing in the kitchen. Dad was probably still in bed or already gone for work. Today was a great day to walk around the beach since it was the weekend. The only friend that I had was Collin. Our parents worked on the same police force, so I knew he had something planned for us.

I rolled out of bed and headed down the stairs. Noting prepared me for what I was seeing. It had to be at least twelve police officers in our living room. I didn't know what was going on, but it couldn't be good. The only time that they come together like this is if one of their fellow officers gets hurt. Still in my pajamas I went looking for my parents. I began to panic walking into each room of the house.

"Are you ok pretty lady?" officer Shabez asked me.

"I'm looking for my parents. Where are they?"

"Oh, they are out back. She is keeping him out there, so we can surprise him," he replied.

"Surprise him for what?"

"He's getting a medal of honor today. Your mom didn't tell you?"

Folding my arms, I replied, "No, she never tells me anything."

"Awe it's ok. How about you give it to him. I was going to do it, but I think he would love it more if it came from his little girl."

"That's ok," I said with a sad face." My mom never really let me in on things concerning my dad. Today was a big day for him and she didn't even tell me.

I went into the kitchen and it was a lot of food on the big table. Looking on the stove there wasn't even any breakfast. All the foods she cooked were what they ate for parties. Glancing at the clock it was only twelve. I was hungry and had I touched any of the food I was sure to get in trouble. I ran back up stairs and took a shower. I wasn't even going to stick around. Nobody bothered to inform me on what was going on so why should I stay? After I took my shower I texted Collin to see where he was.

"Hey punk, what are you doing?"

"Nothing just got out the shower. What are you up too?"

"Trying to leave. You know my mom is having a party for my dad and didn't even tell me?"

"What?" he replied with a puzzled face emoji. "Why she ain't tell you?"

"Man, I don't know. Its cool though. I'm getting dressed now. Are we still meeting up like we always do?"

"Yeah, we can. Don't you think you should stay there though? I think your dad would be very upset if you weren't there for him."

"He will be ok, he wont even know I'm gone. All his police buddies are here and their wives. Aint no other kids here, so why should I stay."

"I don't know. Well I'll be at the beach in about thirty minutes. Meet me by the old shack."

"Ok."

Collin and I have been friends for a couple of years. I met him at one of my dads dinners. His dad left the police force after a really bad injury. He was cute with a kind of rugged look to him. Smile was to die for, plus he was a sweet heart. Our parents always would try to say that we liked each other, but Collin wasn't my type. I had my eye on another guy that I seen at the beach.

Once I had gotten dressed I heard a really loud shout coming from down stairs. It startled me, so I went to go see what it was. Racing down the stairs my heart was racing. When I made it to the bottom of the stairs my parents were hugging each other. I was scared for I had though something happened.

"Victoria!" my dad yelled with excitement. "Come see this award I just received." I walked over to him and grabbed the award out of his hands.

"It looks nice dad; congratulations," I replied with a smile. I gave him a really big hug and a kiss.

"Are you staying for the party before I have to go to work?" he asked.

"Yeah, I will stay for a little bit. I was going to meet Collin at the beach in a few it that's ok?"

"Yeah that's fine honey. Just don't stay out too long ok," he replied giving me a really big hug and a kiss.

My mother was standing there looking at me all crazy. I knew she had an issue. I loved my dad more than anything. I hated the fact that he was never home, so I had to deal with my nagging mother all the time. I walked around speaking to all of my dads friends. They all looked up to him. they always had these little parties and I would have to talk to everyone. Walking into the kitchen I saw my dad's friend Officer Shabez. He was making him something to eat. He was always nice to me.

"Hey pretty lady, did get you something to eat?"

"No sir, not yet. I'm not really hungry."

"Awe is everything ok?" he asked putting his hand on my shoulder.

"Yes sir," I replied. "What did my dad do for him to receive his award?"

"He has been with our force way before you were born. He does an amazing job; we all look up to him." I just stood there listening. "When you were born your dad asked me to watch out for you if anything was to happen to him."

"Really? So, your like my uncle?"

"Yeah something like that."

"Oh, ok. Well I have to go."

"Ok little lady. You be careful out there, so your dad and I won't have to come looking for you."

We both laughed, and he gave me a hug. I knew my dad had people watching me, but I didn't know it was that serious. It was refreshing to know that my father loved me enough to keep me safe. When I walked out the kitchen I ran into my mother. She didn't look to happy.

"So where do you think your going?" she asked with an attitude.

"I was going to the beach to meet up with Collin," I replied.

"Don't you see that were having a celebration for your father?"

"Yeah, but he said I could go."

"And I said you couldn't, so tell Collin you will meet him some other time." I folded my arms and I made a loud huff noise. All of my dad's friends started looking at me funny.

"But mom."

"Don't but mom me. I said you can't go and I mean it."

I swear that woman irked my last nerve. She always knew how to suck the fun out of my life. I was fifteen almost sixteen and I felt like a prisoner. I sat in the living room the whole time and didn't budge. I couldn't wait to move out on my own.

*** FLASHBACK OUT***

Chapter Eleven: Money Moves

Ж

Being here in Miami was amazing. I was meeting a lot more people and doing a lot more modeling jobs. Collin and I were still not married yet, and I haven't even cared to say anything. I was keeping in touch with Mr. Santiago and he had some promising plans for me. I was ready to spread my wings. Things between Camron and I were getting weird. It was like he felt as if we were in a relationship now.

It had been a few weeks since the parties, and I was sure that he would call me for another job. I hate waiting on people. Collin was picking up more and more work, so he wasn't going home anytime soon. I had some time to do what it was I needed to do, just incase he wanted to bolt on me. Our sex life was ok, but I still craved other men. Camron was the only other guy I slept with, but even he wasn't enough. I had my eyes on some new fun and I was bound to get it.

I had my week planned out for much needed fun and pleasure. Being friends with Jazmine had it's perks. She knew so many people and this week we was going to New York for a job. Even though I wasn't working I was going just to enjoy myself. Collin wasn't too happy about me leaving, but it wasn't his decision.

Packing up my things to leave I couldn't help but to think more and more about Mr. Santiago. His body was calling me, and he just did something to my body that made melt. I just had to see him, and I didn't want to leave without seeing him. Once I was done gathering all my clothes I texted Jazmine to let her know I would be ready in about an hour. Our plane was to leave in three hours, so I had just enough time to have a little bit of fun. I knew exactly what to do.

"Hey sweetie are you busy today?" I asked Mr. Santiago.

"Hey Victoria. No, I'm not busy; What's going on?"

"Well, I was leaving with Jazmine today and was wondering if I could come see you."

"Where yawl going?"

"New York. She has a job there for a week, and I'm going with her."

"Oh, ok. Yeah, I definitely need to see you then before you leave me. A week is too long for me not to see your pretty face."

"Awe, you gone miss me?"

"Hell yeah! Your too pretty not to miss. Where are you now?" he asked.

"I'm at home. Can you come pick me up right now?"

"Yeah, shoot me your address and I'll be on my way."

"It's 765 163rd ave. I will be standing outside waiting on you."

"Ok your not that far. I will be there in ten minutes."

I was grinning from ear to ear. I was glad Collin had already left for work, and I was about to enjoy my week. Standing outside waiting for Mr. Santiago to show up, Camron pulled up. I was in no mood to hear what he had to say. Rolling down his passenger window I rolled my eyes and walked down three of our stairs.

"What's going on beautiful?"

"Nothing, what are you doing here?"

"I wanted to see you, is that a crime?"

"Yeah, when you don't tell me you coming."

"I mean damn do you have somewhere to be?" he asked putting the car in park and getting out.

"Yeah, a mater-of-fact I do have somewhere to be somewhere." As soon as I said that Mr. Santiago pulled up. "Oh, and here's my ride."

"You just gone walk away?" he said as I was going towards the car.

"Yes, I have to go. Now if your done I would like for you to leave."

"No! I'm not done talking to you Victoria!" he said grabbing at my arm.

"Is everything ok?" Mr. Santiago said getting out of his car.

I swear I felt like I was watching a wild wild west standoff. They were looking at each other with a stare in their eyes trying to figure each other out.

"Come on," I aid pushing Mr. Santiago back into his car.

"Camron, I have to go," I said walking past him getting into the passenger side of the car. "I will call you later ok."

"Man whatever," he replied pissed off.

"Who was that clown?" Mr. Santiago asked. I could tell he was very upset at me. He had a mean mug on his face.

"That's the guy I work for."

"Why was he there? Did you tell him about me?"

"No, I don't even know why he showed up. I don't even want to work with him anymore."

"Then why are you still dealing with him?"

"Because I have bills to pay."

"Well you work for me now," he said placing his hand on my thigh.

"Oh, do I now?"

"Yeah. I don't want you around him anymore!"

I looked down at my hands wondering what I was about to get myself into. This man wanted me, and he wanted me bad. I was thinking to myself if I wanted to move forward with him or go back and deal with Camron. When we pulled up to his nice house again. All of the things I was thinking went out my head. I was about to be taken care of just how I wanted and wasn't nobody about to get in the way of that.

When we pulled up into his driveway he got out and came to my side of the car and opened the door. I haven't had a guy do that for me in years. I felt like royalty. He was

SECRETS OF AN UNFAITHFUL LOVER 2

already wining me over. I haven't even gave him none of my goodies yet and he was making me feel tingly inside. Going into his house we went into his living room. Still amazed at all the things he had I started to envision myself living with. He walked behind me and started rubbing on my shoulders.

"So how do you like it here in Miami?" he asked.

"I like it a lot here. I'm glad that I came."

"I'm glad you came too. Now we can have some fun."

"What kind of fun?" I asked grabbing on to his hands melting from his nice touch on my neck. He then began to run his hands through my hair.

"You can have all the fun you want as long as you belong to me and me only." In that moment I wasn't even thinking about Camron or Collin. Neither of them was giving me what I needed so I had to agree to get my way.

SECRETS OF AN UNFAITHFUL LOVER 2

"I'm all yours baby. Just promise me you won't hurt me," I said going along with his plan.

"Oh baby. I will never hurt you. I want to take care of you. I want you by my side every step of the way. Your my pawn."

"Pawn? What does that mean?"

"Let's just say once I start showing you off. We will be making more money than ever before."

I wasn't sure if I was ok with what I was hearing, but if he was insuring that was going to make money than I was all for it. I couldn't turn back now. He was already kissing me on my neck. I wasn't about to stop him either. He work his hands down to my breast and caressed them like he never felt some before.

My mind started going everywhere. I knew that I was going to get him hooked too. I pulled him to the front of me and I made him kiss me. His lips were soft like velvet, and he made my knees weak. I couldn't stop

touching on his soft chest. Unbuttoned his shirt and taking

off his pants I was ready to secure my job. It was now or

never. Either I was going to chase my dreams or run back

to Rio with my tail between my legs.

He laid me down on his creamed colored sofa and

lifted up my shirt. His eyes widen with happiness and he

began to smile.

"You sure you want to do this," he asked before he

slid off my bra.

"Yes, I want to. I'm a kid you know. I can handle

it," I replied in anticipation.

"I know your not a kid," he laughed. "I just want to

make sure you really want to do this."

"Just hush and kiss me. Your doing too much

talking," I said pilling him closer to me.

Letting him take off my clothes my body shivered with weakness. I wanted him so damn bad. He stood up in front of me and took off his clothes. His body was too sexy. Muscles in all the right places, and his cologne lingered in the air. I closed my eyes letting him know that I was ready. Just when I though he was about to slide himself inside me.

He lifted my legs up to my head. It had been a long time since my pussy was tasted. I wasn't nervous, but I was because I wasn't sure how well he knew how to do it. With my eyes still closed he began running circles around my clit with his tongue. The fact that Collin never done it before and Camron was bad at it. I felt like I was in heaven. He was a pro at what he was doing. For ten minutes he had his head between my legs like I was a gourmet meal.

My mind was at ease just for that moment. I needed the release. He placed a condom on then slid himself inside me. I pulled back because it hurt a tad bit, but then he was sliding in and out of me with grace. Holding onto his ass pushing him inside me deeper and deeper I was felling the sexual attraction. We both moaned together enjoying the aroma of our sweat. Kissing and rubbing every inch of each other. I knew he wasn't going to let me walk away easy. I was already hooked, and from the way he was inside of me I knew he was enjoying himself too. He started going in and out of me faster and faster. My moaning got even louder. I didn't care who heard me. I was getting fucked just like I liked it. In that moment we both came at the same time. Our breathing was impaired for a moment as he laid on my chest trying to catch his breath.

"Damn girl, you got some good ass pussy," he said looking me in my face. I was not use to all this attention.

"I enjoyed you too."

"I don't know what I'm going to do with you," he said lifting off of me.

"You can do what ever you want with me," I replied not realizing what I was saying until it rolled off my tongue. He looked at me with shock.

"Oh really? So, you're ready for this rollercoaster?"

"I guess so."

He stood up and put his clothes back on as well I. going into my purse to check the time I noticed that I had a few missed calls. Most of them were from Camron and the rest were from Jazmine and Collin. I texted Jazmine and told her that I would be ready in an hour, and I told Collin I was about to board my plane. He didn't even text back, but Jazmine told my ass to hurry up. I'm sure she had a clue what was talking me so long, but hey I had to get my fix before we left.

I told Mr. Santiago that I had to leave so that I could go on my trip. He wasn't too happy about it, but I couldn't pass it up. He understood better than anybody about following dreams, so he took me back home. Before I got out of his car he gave me the longest kiss ever. It felt like forever. Collin never kissed me like he did. What was he trying to prove? What was he hinting at? He had feeling so tingly inside. I started not to get out the car, but Jazmine pulled up behind us.

"I got to go sweetie. My ride is here. We have a flight to catch soon."

"Do you really have to go?" he whined.

"Yes, I promise I will call you as soon as I get back. I will be gone for a week."

"Call me as soon as you get there, and I will have a surprise for you when you get back."

He handed me a rolled up wod of cash kissed me goodbye and I got out. I thanked him and went into the house to get my things. Jazmine came in behind me and helped me grab my bags.

"Girl, so you know you have to tell me everything!"

"About what?" I replied acting as if I didn't know what she was talking about.

"You and William don't play with me. Spill it what's up."

"Oh, nothing is going on. He stopped by to ask me to work for him."

"Well, are you?"

"I don't know yet. I'm still in contract with Camron. He came by here today mad as hell too."

"Girl get out of that while you still can. I worked for him for three months, and I just couldn't do it anymore. You wont make any money with him."

"See that's what I'm saying. I need my coins and if he wont provide that then I can't work with him."

"Girl plus I heard his dick was little," she said demonstrating how little it was with her fingers. I couldn't do nothing but laugh.

"Girl shut up!" I yelled. But she was right. It was small, but it was wide as hell. Having sex with him for as long as I was. I really didn't pay it no attention. He just satisfied me when Collin didn't.

"We have to hurry up though. I don't want to miss our flight. You ready to have some fun?"

"Hell yeah!"

The air port was only thirty minutes away from where I loved. I had never been anywhere, so this was going to be fun. I was glad that I was going with Jazmine because she knew everyone. Getting cool with her at this time was perfect. We boarded our plane and we were on our way.

Chapter Twelve: Welcome To New York

Ж

"Everyone please remain in your seats. We are now arriving in New York City," the flight attendant said over the intercom.

We were flying in first class. It only took us three hours to get here, and I slept the whole way. It was something about flying that made me very sleepy. I guess it was soothing. Jazmine was too turnt. She was happy and loud hitting letting me know we were about to land.

This was like a dream come true for me. I have always wanted to travel the world and today was the beginning of my new life. As we were landing I started to feel really funny. It was kind of like I had to throw up, but it wouldn't come up. I put my head between my legs to see if it would work. I had read on the internet that's what you had to do.

"Girl are you ok?" Jazmine asked laughing at me.

"No! I feel sick," I replied still holding my head between my legs.

"Awe you will be ok. You will get the hang of flying fucking around with me. I'm always traveling."

"It's not funny Jazmine."

The plane started to land, and everyone began to gather their things. I was glad we weren't in the air anymore. I swear this happened when we moved from Rio. I was excited though. I was in a whole other state far away from Collins boring ass. Just like Miami I felt like I was in heaven. New York was busy. I saw more people here than I imagined I would.

"Come on girl so we can catch a cab to the hotel. I have a show later on tonight, but I wasn't to eat first."

"Ok cool. Girl thanks for letting me tag along. I was going to be bored with Camron all week. You know how he is."

"Speaking of Camron. What did you tell him when you said you was coming with me? He didn't try to stop you from coming?" she asked waving her hand in the air for a cab.

"Girl I don't even want to think about him. Even if he was mad I wouldn't care. He ain't my man nor my daddy."

"Damn girl ok. Shit I'm sorry you know how he can be though."

"Yeah, he was too mad I left him standing in my front yard this morning." Still trying to get a cab, I texted Mr. Santiago and told him that we landed. His message back made me want to have him here.

"He will get the picture."

I wasn't trying to play him too bad. After all we did have history, and he did give me a job when I first got to Miami. After finally getting a cab we were on our way. I was anxious to see what kind of jobs Jazmine had to do for a whole week. She made a few phone calls on our ride to the hotel. I was still texting Mr. Santiago.

"Do you miss me yet?" I asked him seeing what answer he would give me.

"Hell yeah! What hotel are you going to be at?"

"I'm not sure, why what's up?"

"I was just asking. When you get there let me know."

"Ok, I will." Right in the middle of me texting him back Collin called. I was hesitant to answer, but I didn't want him getting suspicious either. So, I answered it.

"Hey babe," I said trying to be discreet.

"Hey love. Did you make it to New York safe and sound?"

"Yea, we about to go to the hotel now."

"Where are you staying in New York?"

"Manhattan," I replied. I wasn't sure why he was asking so many questions, but I knew he wasn't doing to show up, so I told him.

"Oh ok, you're in the good parts I pray. Please be careful. Call me later on tonight before you go to bed."

"Ok Collin I will," I said lying just to get him off the phone. I hung up immediately.

"Girl who was that?"

"Oh, that was my boyfriend."

"Wait, what you mean your boyfriend? You never told me you had a boyfriend."

"You never asked either," I replied not even the bit of interested in talking about him.

"So how long yawl been together?"

"Jazmine really? I don't want to talk about him at all ok?"

"Ok girl, anyway. Do you still plan on working with Camron? What's up with you and him?"

"Nothings up. I just wanted him to help me become a model. Now it's like he wants to be more than just coworkers. I guess it's a business thing they got going on because Layla and Kenny are fucking. So, I guess that's how they keep their girls. I mean I fucked Camron a few times, but I just wanted something better; you know?"

"Yeah girl I understand. Camron and Kenny tried to get me to have a threesome with them. I guess they figured since I was already a model and needed money that would get me to work with them. I swear guys feel like money rules us. I make my own money and I will not fuck anybody to get it; you know what I mean?"

"Yeah; I feel you on that."

I was looking down at my hands the whole time we rode around looking for a great hotel. She had no idea what plan I had in mind for myself. I didn't care how I got the money nor who it was coming from. I needed to make sure I had everything that I needed.

Since Collin and I moved to Miami I had saved up over seven thousand dollars. He still don't know that I have it. Between him throwing me cash and Camron giving me money. I can honestly say I am living my life the way I wanted. My father is probably turning over in his grave right now, but a woman has to make a living. We had finally made it to the hotel they paid for in order for Jazmine to dance. It was amazing just on the outside.

"We here girl," Jazmine yelled in my ear.

"Good, I'm ready for a shower and some fun."

"Well, you have your own room that I paid for. So, you can have all the privacy you want. We are in New York, so enjoy yourself."

"Are you serious girl? You know I'm about to have a ball with you. This is the only other place I've been since we moved from Rio."

"Turn the fuck up friend!"

We walked into the Plaza Hotel. I was so shocked how big and amazing this place looked. Everybody who was rich famous or had a lot of money was here. I couldn't believe my eyes. I felt like I was in a movie or something. The receptionist was very nice as she gave us the keys to our rooms. I was just in heaven. I knew this week was going to be the best. Our rooms were right across the hall from each other.

"Girl I just seen a huge pool, I am going to take a swim while you handle your business."

"Enjoy it, I have to meet up with my boss in a few. I will call you when it's time for us to leave."

"Thanks again girl for letting me tag along," I said as I was opening my room door.

"Girl no problem."

Going into my room I plopped on the bed. It was all mine and I didn't have to share it with anyone. I rolled around in it messing it up for about five minutes before I went down to the pool area. Since I didn't have a bathing suit I just had on a nice bra and some shorts. I couldn't pass up this moment alone. I was living the life, even though these moments were given to me by my friend. I didn't want this week to go any faster.

Chapter Thirteen: The Mix-Up
Ж

A couple of days had passed, and we were having a great time in New York. We went shopping and to a party for one of her modeling friends. I swear I felt like I was living my best life. Couldn't nothing spoil my moment. It was about nine in the morning when I heard a knock on my room door.

"Who is it?" I yelled from my bed not waning to get out of it. I had a really bad hangover from last night.

"Room service ma'am." I stretched and pulled the covers off of me.

"*I didn't order any room service,*" I said to myself. "Um, I didn't order any room service," I repeated walking to the door.

"It's complementary of the hotel, and your friend Jazmine told me to get you ready for today."

166

"Get me ready?" "Um, ready for what?" I asked with concern.

"Ma'am I was just told to get ready. I'm not sure of all the details." I opened the door. It was a short older woman standing there with a bag and lots more stuff. I let her in.

"So, Jazmine planned something for us tonight you said?"

"Yes ma'am. I am to do your hair makeup and help you find a nice dress to ware," she said placing her things on the table.

I was in total shock. What in the hell did Jazmine have up her sleeves? The woman started on my hair and makeup first. It was soothing because she gave me small little massages in between. I had never in my life experienced anything this amazing. I was glad I came

SECRETS OF AN UNFAITHFUL LOVER 2

because I was going to renege on her and stay back with Mr. Santiago.

After getting all sexy and finding the perfect dress. A call came to my room letting me know that my limo was outside waiting for me. My mouth dropped and all I could say was ok. What was this girl doing? She sure was trying her best to show me a good time. I texted Mr. Santiago to tell him about the what was going on, but he never texted me back. I thought that was pretty strange, but I just let it go.

I was about to have a nice dinner with my friend and nobody was going to spoil it. I also texted Jazmine and told her that I was at the nice restaurant waiting on her and she didn't respond either. I was clueless on what the hell was going on. Walking into the Marea I was stunned; this place was stunning and looked way out of my budget and hers. I texted her back again and she still didn't respond.

"Reservation?" the man asked as soon as I reached the podium.

"Um, I'm not sure who's name its under. My name is Victoria and I was asked to come here," I told him hoping he would tell me what was going on.

"Oh yes, right this way ma'am," he replied. I didn't know what was going on.

This place was beyond my budget. Nobody was texting me back, so I had a bad feeling about all if this. Walking to my seat my palms began to sweat. The couples that were eating looked so happy. I was all alone. I wished Jazmine would hurry up and get here.

"This place is nice," I said still following the gentlemen to my table.

"Here's your table ma'am," he said pulling out my chair for me.

"Thanks."

"Can I get you something to drink? Like some wine or champagne to start with?"

"I will have a glass of white wine please," I replied. I have always wanted to try it and feel like I was important. Important and rich people drink wine and eat caviar.

"One glass of white wine coming right out ma'am," he said before giving me the small menu to look over.

Sitting there in my pretty red dress with my long black hair bone straight. I was looking beautiful, but yet and still I was sitting alone. I was confused and sad at the same time. Why would someone do something like this in a city I wasn't familiar with. I sat drinking on my wine thinking if I should leave or stay and eat.

"Did you decide on your meal ma'am?"

"Yes, I might as well enjoy my night. No sense of wasting a good time, right?"

"I was going to say the same thing," he said smiling at me.

"I'll have the steak; medium rare and mashed potatoes. I will also have some asparagus and some buttered shrimp."

"Would that be all ma'am?"

"yes, that will do for now. Oh, and another glass of wine please."

"Coming right up ma'am."

"Thank you." Waiting on my food to come I texted Jazmine again to see what the hold up was. "Hey girl are you meeting me at the restaurant?" I asked with multiple question marks.

"My bad girl I was with my boss. What restaurant? I didn't know we were supposed to have dinner tonight."

"Yes, you did. You had the hotel get me ready and now I'm here waiting on you."

"I didn't have the hotel set up anything. I have no clue what you talking about girl."

"So, your telling me that you didn't have me come to this expensive place alone?"

"Victoria, I have no clue what you are talking about girl. Maybe it was a mix-up." I called her immediately because this was a horrible joke.

"Jazmine this has to be a joke," I said trying not to scream on the phone.

"Vic, I didn't have the hotel do anything. Ask the waiter what's going on."

"He obviously knows what's going on because I had to give him my name when I walked in. And the lady from this morning said you had her come get me ready. I just want to know what the hell is going on."

"Friend I have no clue. I have been busy working all day. I just got out of my meeting. What you gone do?"

"Here comes the waiter now. I'll call you back." I said before hanging up. "Sir are you able to tell me who brought me here?" I asked. As soon as I asked him Mr. Santiago came walking in right behind him. My mouth dropped. "What are you doing here?" I asked standing up to greet him with a hug.

"I wanted to surprise you and show you how well you would be treated being with me," he replied. I was in total shock. Collin has never done nothing like this for me.

"But they said Jazmine set this up for me."

"Yeah I know. I had to come up with something, so you wouldn't find out it was me. Are you happy?"

"Yes, yes I am very happy. How long are you going to be here?"

"For as long as you want me to be. I really don't want you in this city alone anyway."

"That's so sweet of you. Do you do this for all the girls you want?"

"No, not all girls are special to me. You deserve the best and I'm here to make sure that happens." In the far back of my head I started to think about Collin. I know I told him that I would be a good girl, but who in their right mind would pass all this up? "Is everything ok? You look a little upset."

"I'm fine," I lied. "I'm still taking all this in. Nobody goes out of their way to make sure I'm happy. Plus, I just don't want this night to end."

"Who said it had to?"

I was beyond happy. My food arrived, and he had already pre-ordered his. We sat there listening to the soft music and enjoying each other company. I was enjoying the fact that he stooped at nothing to get my attention. He came all the way from Miami to surprise me, and he went great lengths to make sure the surprise wasn't ruined. I couldn't stop smiling. I had more wine and had some desert. The way I was feeling tonight couldn't get any better.

After dinner we took a nice long ride in the limo. I felt like a princess being rescued by her prince charming. Mr. Santiago was really doing everything that I wanted in a mad. Hell, he had everything a man was supposed to have. While with him Collin called me, but I declined his call. I wasn't going to let anyone mess this up for me.

Chapter Fourteen: The Bad Deal

Ж

It was the last two days of our trip in New York. I didn't see much of Jazmine for being with Mr. Santiago the whole time. I know she was upset at me, but I really had rather been with him than to tag along with her. We attended a few of her shows, but we wanted to paint the town.

I woke up this morning with a feeling of sadness hanging over me. I wasn't really sure what it was, but it couldn't have come at a worse time. Mr. Santiago was lying right next to me sound asleep, and Collin was texting me. He was asking so many questions and was concerned. He also wanted me to call him. I didn't want to roll out of the bed and wake up Mr. Santiago.

Trying to slide out the bed to sneak to the bathroom; Mr. Santiago grabbed me and pulled me closer to him. I was trying to move again but I ended up dropping my phone on the floor. It made a really loud noise and he jumped up.

"What was that?"

"Nothing, it was nothing go back to sleep," I lied.

"Come here baby. I need to feel you." I rolled over leaving my phone on the floor. "I had a great time with you last night. You really outdid yourself last night."

"I didn't do anything that you didn't want me to do. Did you sleep well?"

"Yeah, knowing that I was laying next to you. What do you want to do today?" he asked rubbing on my ass.

"I was thinking I would meet up with Jazmine since we will only be here for a couple more days. Is that ok with you?"

"I mean I came all the way out here to be with you and now you want to leave me alone to go play with your stripper friends?"

"It's not like that, I mean she did pay for me to come out here. I can't just not show my support." He threw me off of him with anger. After last night I thought he would at least understand.

"When you are ready to grow up call me. I don't have time to play these childish games with you Victoria." He began to put on his clothes.

"I don't understand why you are so angry. You knew I was coming out here to help her. I was here for her support."

"What does a grown ass woman need support stripping for? She's a fucking dancer and a lousy one at that!" he yelled.

"Keep your voice down William. She still my friend. I cant just leave her hanging." I wasn't sure why he was acting like a baby. Maybe I shouldn't have put it on him that good last night. I was just showing my appreciation. "Let me just go check on her ok baby. I just need to make sure she is good. We came out here together."

"Yeah, ok I guess. Hurry up. I have another surprise for you."

"You don't have to keep giving me gifts sweetie. I will be right back."

Putting on my robe and slippers I left the room to go check on Jazmine. But before I even knocked on her door I went to the stairwell. Puling my phone from my robe pocket that I swiped off the floor before leaving. I was getting really frustrated and I needed my nerves to be settled, so I called the one person that I knew could make that happen.

"Hello," Collin said answering the phone with happiness.

"Hey baby. I miss you so much."

"I miss you too baby. When are you coming home love? I miss you so much. The house is too quiet and empty without you here."

"I'll be home soon I promise," I said with tears running down my face. What the hell was I doing? Was money and sex more important? "I have to finish up here with Jazmine then I will be on the first flight home," I explained to him.

"Ok baby I love you. Enjoy the rest of your trip," he said before hanging up the phone.

I sat there with tears running down my face like a stream. At home I had a man who wanted me and adored me since we were kids. And in my hotel room I had a man who wouldn't mind giving me the world. Then there was

Camron; a man who knew things that I have done that will destroy my whole world. With my tail between my legs like a puppy. I couldn't go into Jazmine's room like this, so I got myself together before going to check on her. I was already gone too long. William would be on his way out trying to regulate. I knocked on her door trying not to be too loud.

"Who is it?" she yelled.

"It's me Victoria," I replied. She opened the door fully dressed pretty and ready to paint the town.

"Look at you all sexy," I said walking into her room.

"Girl thank you. Are you ready to go to the grand ball?"

"That's what I came to talk to you about. I was wondering if I could bring a plus one with me?"

"But your my plus one," she said laughing.

"I know but William showed up and I don't want to leave him alone."

"William? You mean William from the party?"

"Yeah, we kind of have a thing going on," I said trying not to fully explain.

"So, you been seeing him?" she said putting on her earrings.

"Yeah something like that. You know I have a man at home, but he wasn't trying to let me walk away that day. Then he keeps throwing me cash and I cant give that up."

"Girl you don't have to explain to me. I have a man at home too. Us women have to do what we have to do to survive. Now I'm not going to tell you what your doing is wrong, but I will tell you to be careful."

"I know, it's just something about money that makes me not have a care in the world. I love my fiancé but he's not doing what I need him to financially. William on

182

SECRETS OF AN UNFAITHFUL LOVER 2

the other hand does everything I want and need in a man. Am I wrong?"

"Girl no your not wrong. Your living your best life. You are young and only have one life to live." I looked up at her and she was dead serious. I didn't know what to think. Was I supposed to believe her or just stop now? "All that matter is your making money, and money makes everyone happy."

"You ain't lying. You never said if I could bring him or not," I reminded her before I left her room.

"Girl yeah you can bring him. We can double date afterwards too."

"Ok girl. I'll let him know. Don't be trying to show me up tonight either," I said laughing.

"Girl you know I got the juice. Naw I'll make sure we both looking sexy." I walked away laughing.

I was loving the fact Jazmine and I was as cool as we were. She was like a sister to me. Being the only child, I couldn't bond with anyone else. She was the sister I needed. With a little bit of relief, I went back to my hotel room. When I opened the door felt a hand slap me in my face. I help my tight with tears falling from my eyes.

"What took you so fucking long," he yelled him my face.

"I was talking to Jazmine," I replied sobbing.

"Bitch it don't take thirty minutes to tell some stripper that you won't be attending shit with her!" he said still yelling and pointing his finger in my face.

"But William, we are supposed to be her guest at her show tonight."

"We? We who?"

"Me and you! She said for both of us to come and show her some love."

"I didn't come to see her. I came all the way out here to show you a good time. Now either you get your ass up off that bed and pack your shit, or I will pack it for you."

I balled myself up on the bed holding my legs up to my chest. I was so confused. This man was so sweet when we first me. He showed me that he knew how to treat a woman. Now it's like he was changing into a different person. I didn't understand why he was so angry, nor did I see that he had a bad side to him.

"Can we please go to the party tonight Collin? I mean William." I buried my head into my knees hoping that he dint hear me.

"What the fuck did you say!" he yelled forcing me to look at him.

"I can I please go to the party."

"You said Collin! Who the fuck is Collin?" he asked with the angriest face I had ever seen. It was like the devil himself was present.

"I didn't say that William. I just said that I wanted to go to the party that's all," I said trying not to make him even madder.

"Get your shit on and come on right now!"

"I don't want to leave yet." He walked up to me. He stood there just staring at me. He was looking at me like he wanted to do something, but he didn't. "You have one second to get your ass off that bed!" Before I could say anything, he yanked me up into his arms. "Don't make me tell you again!"

"Ok William let me put my clothes on," I said so he would stop tripping. At this point I was rethinking this whole situation.

After gathering my things, we left the hotel. I didn't even get to say goodbye to Jazmine. I didn't want to leave without her since we had came together. Catching the cab to the airport and catching the next flight back to Miami. He was holding my arm tight the whole time we waited to board our flight. Looking at him I knew this was going to be a big issue. After an hour of waiting we boarded our flight.

"When we get off this plane I want you to go home and pack the rest of your shit. Your moving in with me."

"Why?" I asked in fear.

"Because I said so." I put my head down to let my eyes rest. In the back of my mind I was worried about Collin. How was I supposed to just up and leave him like that? "And your cutting of Jazmine too," he said holding on to my arm." I just dozed off and went to sleep until we landed.

Chapter Fifteen: Fighting For Love

Ж

"Victoria, where are you?" Collin asked when he called my phone this morning an leaving a message. He had called my phone a bunch of times already. "Please baby call me back baby; I am really worried about you," he said on another one.

I couldn't believe myself just leaving him like this. William was so angry at me for wanting to stay in New York with Jazmine. She also called me a few times. I didn't know what to do. William was talking control over everything. I couldn't even use the bathroom without him knowing. It wasn't until now that what I was doing was going to cost me everything.

Waking up laying in his bed naked and cold. My body and face was in a lot of pain. I went into the bathroom that was adjacent to his room. When I looked at myself in the mirror my was black and my cheek was swollen. In the back of my head I was making excuses for him, and I know he didn't mean it. But this was not what I signed up for, nor was it ok. Cleaning my face before William woke up, I was trying to figure out how to sneak out. Collin had been calling me all morning, so I turned the shower on to call him back. Before I called I locked the door, so William wouldn't come in. Sitting on the toilet I dilled Collins number. My legs were shacking, and my mind was racing.

"Hello, Collin," I said whispering.

"Hey baby, where are you? I have been calling you all morning. I went to the airport to get you, but you never came out. Is everything ok?" he asked with concern.

"Yes, baby I'm fine. We had to stay for a couple more days," I lied. I didn't want him to be worried, and I could tell he already was. "I will be home soon I promise. How's everything there?"

"It's going. I miss you a lot though. Its way too quiet here." As we talked William started banging on the door.

"I have to go baby I will call you tomorrow," I said trying to rush him off the phone.

"Wait Victoria! Who was that? What's going on?"

"Collin, I have to go, I love you," I said rushing to hang up. I took off all my clothes and got into the shower.

"Victoria! Open this fucking door right now!" he yelled.

"I'm in the shower baby hold on I have soap in my eyes!" Reaching out the shower for a towel; I went to open the door. "Hey baby, I'm sorry you were sleep so I thought I would take a shower," I lied.

"Do I look stupid to you? Who were you talking to?"

"What? I wasn't talking to anyone. I was taking a shower." He looked at me and pushed me out the way. He went into the bathroom searching for whatever. "What's the problem William?"

"You must think I'm stupid."

I went back into the shower to wash off the soap that was dripping from my body. He followed right behind me. Trying not to pay him any attention I rinsed off. With him standing there waiting on me to get out. I was thinking about Collin and what I was doing to him. He was pretty worried about me. I had to find a way to make it back home.

"Are you going to hurry up and get out the shower now?" he yelled.

"I'm getting out now William." This was not what I signed up for. When I got out the shower he was just standing there staring at me. "I'm all clean now baby," I said kissing him on his lips.

"Who else are you sleeping with?" he asked grabbing at my face.

"Nobody baby. I haven't even left house. Please let me go! Your hurting me."

"Don't fucking lie to me!" he yelled again while storming out the bathroom.

I followed behind him to put on my clothes. He left out the room and went down stairs. That's when I decided to pack up my things. I had to get away from him. No matter what I did Collin never put his hands on me. I wasn't sure if it was the alcohol or the drugs.

I found myself drowning in a situation that I caused. I had to get myself out of it. The money was great, and the sex was amazing. But I was starting to realize that all this was not worth it. When I got down stairs William was sitting on the couch with his head to his glass table. He was snorting a line of crack, and I knew things was about to get worse.

"I'm going home William," I said standing in front of him with my bags in my hands.

"What did you just say?" he asked with the residue of the drug round his nose. "Come sit your ass down with me and have a meal."

"No William, I have to go home," I reinforced. He got up so fast that I didn't realize how close he was to my face. "William your high; you need to sit down."

"Where the hell do you think your going?" he asked grabbing at my bags.

"I'm going home. This is not what I signed up for William. All you do is get high."

"So, your trying to leave me huh?"

"I need to go home and take care of some things. I will come back I promise."

"I DON'T WANT YOU TO GO ANYWHERE!"

"William you're over reacting. All I'm doing in going home to check on everything. I said I was coming back." I really was going home to make sure Collin wasn't trying to leave me. I was already gone for far too long. As I was standing there Collin was blowing my phone up, I was glad I had it on vibrate. "So, can I leave now?"

"Sit your ass down Victoria!" he yelled. He then pulled me down to my knees. "It's your turn," he said pointing to the line of coke on the table.

"I don't want any!" I yelled back.

"I said its your fucking turn," he yelled again. The next thing I knew I was looking into the barrel of his gun. "Don't make me pull the trigger. I said it's your turn."

I didn't want to lose my life. His gun was pressed to the back of my head. Looking down at the table and feeling the gun pressed against the back of my head; I snorted the coke. The burning sensation in my nose was unbearable. I leaned back on his recliner and put my head in my knees.

"I should have never even came over here," I mumbled to myself.

"What the fuck did you say?"

"Nothing."

"Come sit next to me baby. We are going to have a great time." I hesitated to get up. "Come on baby. I need to feel you next to me."

I got up and sat next to him on the couch. My life at this point was falling apart. While out doing me and being hurt Collin was at home being a great boyfriend. Looking down at my ring, I knew I was in huge trouble. Today was going to be a long day.

Chapter Sixteen: Devil V.S Angel

Ж

It had been three days since I have been back from New York. Collin called me every day asking me when I was coming home. Each time I came up with, yet another lie to tell him, so he wouldn't worry. Jazmine called me yesterday worried about me too. I lied to her, so she wouldn't get suspicious.

William was supposed to go on a trip with some of his friends, so it was the right time for me to leave. I had still had my bags packed and ready to go. He was upstairs getting ready; while I was happy about getting back home to Collin. I began to understand the importance of being faithful and only be with one person. I wasn't getting any younger, and Colin still hadn't left me. After all that I have done to him, he still stayed.

"Victoria get up here and find my damn shirt I told you put out!" he yelled from the room.

"It's hanging up on the door!" I yelled back at him.

"Baby, I don't see it." I started to feel like his mama. I had been cooking his food, washing his clothes, and cleaning. He even fired his maid. I was feeling trapped. No amount of money was worth this. "Baby come help me; I have to leave in twenty minutes," I ran up the stairs to him, pulled the shirt off the closet door and gave it to him.

"I told you it was on the door."

"Thanks baby see that's why I got you by my side," he said kissing me on my forehead. I smiled like I was happy and enjoyed being with him. "When I get back were going to have a great time."

"Yay fun," I said being sarcastic. My face was still a little bruised from him hitting me, and I didn't want him to pull his gun out on me, so I had to play it cool. "So how long will you be gone baby?"

"For a few days. So, don't get into any trouble while I'm gone, ok."

"I hear you. I will be sitting in here board as usual. I might call Jazmine to come get me, so we can go to the mall." That must have struck a nerve with him because he was right in my face again.

"I told you I didn't want you fucking with her anymore Victoria; I fucking mean it. She is not a good girl. She done been in so much trouble. Why do you think I made you come home with me."

"She is not trouble William. She was the only person who had my back since I been here. Other than you, she's all I have."

"I don't want her back in my house Victoria and I mean it."

"O que você disser. Não posso esperar até você sair," I said under my breath.

"What did you say?"

"Nothing. Your going to be late for your flight baby. I will be here when you get back."

"Ok baby. Come walk me to the car."

We walked outside to his car where he wasn't trying to let me go. He had me tight around my waist as I was pulling away trying to get him to leave.

"Baby, you have to go. I will see you when you get back ok," I said pushing him into the car. The sooner her left the sooner I could leave. He was wasting time knowing he had a flight to catch.

"Ok baby, I will be back soon. Take care of the house," he said after kissing me on the forehead. "I love you." I just stood there. I couldn't say it back.

In the back of my mind I knew that he was going to say that shit. I just smiled and closed his door and watched him pull off. Saying it back would have taken things further than it already was. I was anxious to leave. So, I didn't waste no time in calling a cab. I didn't even tell Collin I was coming. I wanted it to be a surprise.

As soon as William left I was in the next cab smoking. I was ready to go home. From the drinking to the drugs and the beatings; it was high time I left. Before we pulled up to the house I put some makeup on my face to cover up the bruises that William gave me. I didn't want Collin to worry. Him seeing the bruises would have raised suspicion. When we pulled up I paid the cab driver and hauled ass into the house. Damn near leaving my bags on the back seat.

"Collin baby I'm home," I said bursting through the door. He was no where in sight. "Collin baby where are you!" I yelled again.

"Hey baby," he replied coming down the stairs.

"I miss you so much," I said back greeting him with a big hug. As he held me tightly tears started to run down my face.

"What's wrong baby?"

"Nothing, I'm just so happy to see you. That's all. Did you miss me?"

"Yes, I did I missed you very much mi amor."

"Você é um homem incrível e eu te amo tanto. Sinto muito, querida."

"Don't worry about it baby, I love you too. It's going to be ok."

I pulled away from him and walked back down the stairs. I sat on the couch with my head in my hands. I wanted to tell him what was going on; I had to tell him what was going on. I didn't want to hurt him anymore. Even though the money I was getting good, and the sex that

I was getting made me feel amazing. I was loosing myself, and my life was at stake.

"Baby, what is going on?" he asked bending down in front of me holding my hands.

"Baby, it's so much. I don't want you to be disappointed in me. I promise you baby I am not trying to hurt you. And you deserve so much better than me."

"Victoria, what in the world are you talking about baby? Did something happen between you and Jazmine while you was in New York? Did you two have sex or something?" he asked with is brows up. I looked at him in shock. What made him ask that?

"No! I don't even know if we are friends right now. I got really high and a lot of bad things happened," I tried to explain.

"Baby look I don't even care what happen. As long as you are home and safe I am fine with that." He grabbed me and held me close.

I was confused. Here I am about to tell this man I was in New York with another man; and he don't care. I was confused, worried and just blown away. The one time I wanted to be honest with him he didn't want to listen. I tried to tell him again.

"Baby listen there is something I want to tell you."

"Victoria, you were on vacation having fun with your friend. I am glad that you found a friend here that you can do girly things with."

"But baby, it's not that," I tried explaining again.

"Look, I know you had a long trip, so I am going to draw you a bath and make you a nice meal." I couldn't believe what I was hearing.

"You don't have to do all that baby," I said trying to stop him.

"I'll be right back. You just get relax."

As he went upstairs I grabbed my phone out my purse. I wanted to text Jazmine to explain what happened. I really didn't want to lose the one friend that I had here, and it was all my fault. When I went to punch her numbers in William called me. I stepped outside on the porch, so Collin couldn't hear anything.

"Hello?"

"Where the fuck are you Bitch!" he said yelling.

"I am at home with my fiancé where I'm supposed to be," I replied not caring how he felt. Collin didn't care what I did, so I was leaving it in the past. "What do you want?"

"I want you to get your ass back here right now!" he was pissed, but I wasn't about to leave again.

"Look I made a mistake. I am getting married soon. So, I would like it if you would stop calling my phone. I am going back to work with Camron soon," I said lying. In fact, I needed to find me a new job. "I got to go."

I walked back into the house. Collin was standing at the bottom of the stairs staring at me. I just brushed right passed him and went to our bedroom. He had it all nice and romantic with the lights dim, and nice smelling candles burning. He led me to the bathroom and took off all my clothes for me.

As I sat in the tub I just started to feel bead. I closed my eyes and slid my body under the water. I had to change for Collin. He didn't deserve nothing that I was doing to him. He bathed me from head to toe after pulling me out the water. He was always too good to me, I was just to dumb and blind to see it. Once he was done he took me to the bed and made love to me like never before. In that moment I made love to him back for the first time. I was happy, and I knew that it was now that I had to start over. I couldn't go on like I was. I didn't want to lose Collin not now and not like this. I went to bed happier than I have ever been, and so did Collin. He held me so tight and it just felt amazing.

Chapter Seventeen: Fighting For Life

Ж

Woke up this morning feeling as good as I ever been. Collin and I had a wonderful time last night. I was glad that things were subtle and great between us. We made passionate love last night, and I woke up to him holding me close. I couldn't help but to think about all the money that I would be losing out on leaving William alone, but he was just too much. I would rather find a small desk job than to deal with his craziness.

While I was laying in the bed my phone started to buzz. It was just about nine in the morning. When I glanced at it, sure enough it was William. I didn't want to hear what he had to say, nor did I want to see him. I had to get my life back in order. Money and sex was turning me into a girl that I wasn't happy with. My father had to be turning over in his grave right now. After the tenth call; I slid out of the bed and went outside on the porch.

"William, what do you want?"

"So, I go back home because my trip was cancelled, and you are not here! Where are you Victoria?"

"I'm where I'm supposed to be; with my fiancé. I would like it if you stopped calling me too. What we had was fun, but it was a mistake. I enjoyed my time with you, but I cant keep doing this to Collin. He's a good man and he deserves a good wife. So just please leave me alone," I said hoping that he would just let me go.

"You think I'm just going to let you go that easy? I invested in you. I gave you my hard-earned cash to do a job, and I say your job is not done. WHERE THE FUCK ARE YOU!" he screamed.

"Look I don't want anymore of your money. I'm sorry, but I have to go," I said hanging up the phone.

I had to end this, I just couldn't see myself like that no longer. Hiding bruises, drugs, and money from Collin was going a tab bit too far. As I walked back in the house, Collin was standing at the bottom of the stairs with a worried look on his face.

"Hey baby; did I wake you?" I asked walking up towards him landing a kiss on his lips.

"Who were you talking to outside baby?" he asked returning the kiss back.

"Oh, that was Jazmine. We were making up after our argument from yesterday," I lied. I know I was supposed to tell him the truth, but since he didn't want to hear it I didn't care anymore either.

"She called pretty early just to apologize. Is everything ok?" he scolded me.

"Yeah baby; everything is fine. She had a early flight this morning, so I guess she wanted to tell me before she got really busy."

"Oh, ok," he said rubbing at my cheeks. "What's this on your face Victoria?" he asked staring at the greenish purple bruise under my eye. My makeup must have warn off during the night. "What happened Victoria?"

"Nothing baby. I just ran into the door at the hotel. I told you we had gotten really drunk. It will go away, stop worrying so much." Right then and there I could have told him the truth, but at what cost. I couldn't risk losing him too.

"I love you so much," he said holding me tight. "I don't know what I would do if I would ever lose you baby," he said following behind his words with a gentle kiss on my forehead.

"I love you too William…" the name just slipped out of my mouth. Holding my head in his chest. I was praying that he didn't hear what I said.

"Humm? What did you say baby?"

"I said I love you too my big handsome man."

My heart was pounding with fear. I had to really let this William thing go. Even if It meant letting Collin know the truth I had to do it. But it had to be at the right time. We stood there for about three mins just holding each other. I had to figure something out. And with William still calling my phone, I had to figure something out fast.

Collin grabbed be by the hands and led be back up to our bedroom. He made me get back into the bed. I wasn't sure what was going on, but he was being so sweet. As I laid my head on the headboard, he kissed my forehead again.

"I'm going to the store and pick you up some things after I get off work today. I want you to get some rest." He then turned off the lights in the room and turned the tv on low.

"Ok baby," I said thinking of something that I could do in the house while he was gone.

"I am serious Victoria, stay in the house. And if you want you can have Jazmine come to you. Don't leave," he repeated.

"She's out of town babe, remember. I will be fine. Don't worry about me," I said shooing him out the house.

Sitting there thinking how bored I was going to be, I started searching through my phone. Even though Collin didn't mind taking care of me; I still wanted my own money. I tried calling Camron to see if he would let me get my job back, but he didn't answer. He must have still been upset at me for leaving him hanging. I was wrong for how I did things, but I just wasn't getting the cash that I deserved. Telling William to get lost and coming back home to my fiancé was the best thing I did.

After about an hour of lying in the bed; I got up and went outside to sit on the porch. The air was fresh, and the sky was clear. Being in Miami was fun, but I started to miss Rio. I missed the beaches, and the carnivals that we had. Miami had their little parties, but it also revolved around drinking and drugs. I just wanted to have fun. Once I got comfortable I received a phone call; the number wasn't familiar, but all I could think about was if it was a job offer, so I answered.

"Hello?"

"Hello, is this Victoria?" the guy replied on the other end.

"Yes, this is she. How did you get my number?" I asked with confusion.

"Well, my name is Ahmod; I was given your number by one of my business partners. I was calling to offer you a job. That's if your still looking for one." I was shocked and confused. As soon as I said I wanted a job, here's this guy saying he has one for me. "Do you want to come in for an interview? I work for Glamorous Pictures Productions, and I need an assistant."

"Yes, oh my God yes!" I yelled. "Where do I need to come?"

"I need you to come to our eastside location. Do you need me to send you the address?" he asked.

"No, I know where it is. I did a few jobs there before. I will be there in an hour."

I hung up and ran back into the house. I was elated. Here I was worried yet again about money and it fell right in my lap. I went to change into a real nice outfit. Nothing too revealing, but not too old fashion either. I wrote Collin a note letting him know where I was going, I didn't want him to worry; and I told Jazmine the good news as well. She didn't text back, so I just left.

Walking three blocks over to the main streets I hailed for a cab. I was not about to pass this up. Letting the cab driver know where I was going, I fixed my makeup and was on my way. I was so anxious, and ready to start my life over. When I pulled up my I couldn't believe what I was seeing. I felt like this was the real dream, this was the reason I left Rio, and I was sure I was about to catch my big break. When I walked into the building I got confused. It was empty. There was no one in sight. I called the number back.

"Hey, I'm here. There is no one here?" I said confused.

"I know," he replied. Come to the back. Everyone has left already. I am in my office." I walked back to where the offices were, and I still didn't see anyone. I was getting pissed.

"Um, I still don't see anyone," I said again. But he had hung up the phone. I turned around and headed for the front door, but it was locked. "Hello," I called out. But there was still no answer. That's when I seen a light come on in one of the rooms. "Hello, is anybody back there?" I asked with fear. This started to make me feel like the time I was trapped in that cave years ago. I walked towards the lighted room. When I peeked in there was candles and rose petals everywhere. "Collin! Are you in here?"

"No, it's not Collin; it's me." William walked out from behind me and pushed me into the room.

"William! What the hell are you doing?"

"We had a good thing going on and you went and messed it up. You just had to go back to you fiancé."

"William, let me go home and just forget about all this. Just let me go home," I tried to reason with him.

"NO!" he yelled and pushed me down onto the mattress laying on the floor. "You won't be going anywhere no time soon."

"You can't just hold me in here William. Collin will get worried," I said letting him know I still wasn't interested in him.

"Collin? Fuck Collin. You wasn't worried about Collin when you was fucking me and sucking my dick now was you? You wasn't worried about Collin when you were doing drugs and having threesomes with me. Did you tell him about that?"

"Wait I never had a threesome with you William," I said confused and disgusted.

"Next time make sure you know what drugs you are taking."

While he was rambling, I took my phone out my purse. I was trying to be discreet. I dialed numbers on it

217

hoping that I was able to reach someone. As soon as they answered he turned around.

"Help me please! He won't...!" I yelled right before he snatched my phone out my hand.

"What the fuck did you do that for!" he yelled with rage. His face was getting redder.

"William please just let me go!" I pleaded.

He took the phone out of my hands and placed it in his pocket. I began to get worried, scared, and terrified. I done really got myself into some trouble. Collin told me not to leave the house and I should have listened to him. This man is fucking crazy. Should have known by the was acting when we first met. He was too nice, and too willing to give me whatever I wanted.

"You think your real slick; don't you? Why would you do that? Why would you make a phone call? What you don't love me?" he asked upset. I just wanted to go home.

"You wont get away with this William. If I'm not back home soon, people will get suspicious."

"Don't nobody care about you, ain't that what you said?" He placed a bag on the table and started to empty it. "We are going to have so much fun," he said with a creepy smile.

"You won't get away with this," I repeated. People who work here will find me. You will rot in jail you sick sadistic prick!" I yelled. He came towards me and I spit on him. He gave me a death look. "You are going to burn in hell," I said still insulting him.

"No, you are in hell. Now sit back and shut up! I have a little surprise for you."

He pilled out a needle. I wasn't sure what was in it, but I didn't want to find out either. He began to walk towards me with the needle still in his hand. He was pressing the bottom of it so some of the contents would come out. I began to scream. I screamed as loud as my lungs would let me.

"HELP! SOMEBODY PLEASE HELP ME!" I yelled and yelled. He covered my mouth with one hand. "Please let me go," I mumbled under his hand.

"Nobody will ever find you here. This is my building and I am the only one with a key. Your going to be here for a very long time," he said as he stuck the needle right into my thigh. It burned so bad, and as soon as he injected me, my body went limp. "I told you we were going to be together. You shouldn't have left me. I was too good to you," he cried out. After ten mins of him mumbling my vision started to go out. I couldn't yell, move, I couldn't do anything. "I will be back. Don't try any funny business."

As he walked out I started to doze off. The room started to spin, and my head started to hurt. I couldn't feel anything. Before my eyes closed I seen a dark shadow walk past me, but I know it was only the drug he gave me. I was

helpless and scared. What was I going to do now?

Chapter Eighteen: Trusted The Devil

Ж

I don't know how long I was out of it, but my vision was still blurry. Trying to lift my body off the bed to see what was going on, but it was hard. I wasn't sure what he gave me, and I began to get worried. Forcing myself off the bed with my hands still tied behind my back. It was a struggle getting up, but I had to figure out how to get out of this room.

I couldn't believe I got myself into this bull-shit. William was still not back, and I had to find a way out of here. stumbling over everything; I couldn't find anything to get this rope off my wrist. He had taken everything out if the room. Looking for my phone hoping that he left it, but he didn't. I started to panic.

****

Meanwhile Back At Victoria's Place: Collin

"Hello, How may I help you?" the lady at the front desk asked me.

"Yes, my name is Collin and I have an order to pick up."

"Let me check to see if it's ready sir," she replied looking through the flowers on her counter.

"Yes, for a Ms. Victoria, right?"

"Yes, ma'am that's right. They are for my lovely fiancé. She's at home sick and I hope these will make her feel better."

"Flowers always make a woman feel better. Why don't you add some chocolate strawberries with them and some chocolate kisses," the woman recommended.

"That would be a great idea. She loves chocolate and fruit. Thanks so much for all your help."

"You welcome have a nice day."

"You too," I replied back as I was leaving the store.

I couldn't wait to see the look on my babies face when she sees all her little gifts. I called her phone to see if she was still sleeping, but her voicemail picked up.

"Hi, you have reached Victoria. I'm sorry I couldn't come to the phone right now. I must be away from my phone or on another call. Please leave a name, number and a brief message and I will get back with you, adios." Her voicemail always made me smile.

"Hey baby, I'm on my way home. I was just calling to see how you were doing. I will be there real soon Mi amor. I love you."

I love that girl so much that I would do anything for her just to make her happy. She was having a rough time last night. So, I decided to surprise her. Pulling up to the house I noticed that all the lights were off. That was strange. Why would she turn off all the lights. It was just about 8pm. Grabbing her gifts I ran into the house to make sure she was ok.

"Victoria, baby! I have some goodies for you!" I yelled running up the stairs to her. But there was no answer back. I went into the room and it was empty. "Victoria baby, Where are you?" I yelled again running through the house searching for her. *"After I had told her not to leave she did anyway,"* I said to myself. I called her phone again. "Victoria! Where are you? I told you not to leave. I need you to call me as soon as possible." After I waited for her to call back my phone rang. "Hello, Victoria! Where are you.

"She can't come to the phone right now," the man on the other end responded.

"Who the fuck is this and where is Victoria?"

"She's in good hands. I just wanted to let you know myself that she no longer wants to be with you. She was too scared to tell you."

"WHERE IS SHE! Put her on the phone."

"I'm sorry; I don't believe I am able to do that. You see, she and I are about to leave the states. You won't be able to find us," he said with a conspicuous voice.

"William? William what the fuck have you done with Victoria?"

"All that matters is that she is with me." He hung up.

I didn't know what to do, so I called the police. I wasn't sure if she was ok or if it was a stupid ass joke. I worked a few jobs with William, so I gave them the address to his place. I paced back and forth waiting for the police to show up, but time was running out. I had to find my baby and soon. There was a knock at the door. When I opened the door, it was two Miami police officers standing there.

"Sir did you call about your wife missing?"

"Yes, sir I did. I explained that I received a phone call from William a former colleague of mine and he stated he had her."

"Well we went to his place…."

"Did you find her?" I asked cutting him off in mid-sentence.

"No, in fact nobody was there. Not even one car.

"Well Victoria doesn't drive. We just moved here from Rio. She knows nothing about this city."

"Well maybe she went out with some friends and they are doing a silly prank."

"No, that man has her I just know he does!"

"Sir calm down. If she isn't back by tomorrow, you call us, and we will take it from there. Just don't do anything stupid."

I shut the door and knocked the books off the shelf. I told her not to leave and now this smug head ass man is playing on my phone. I called back again, but it was going to voicemail. I went back up stairs to see if had taken anything, but she didn't. That's when I noticed it was a note sticking to her mirror.

"Hey, I know you said not to leave the house, but I got a call for a job interview. I shouldn't be gone for no more than an hour. I'm at Glamorous Pictures Productions on the eastside. I just want to be better and do better. Don't worry I will be home soon as I'm done. Love your fiancé Victoria."

I was happy she went for a job interview, but something still wasn't sitting right with me. Something inside told me to go see what was going on, and why she still wasn't home yet. I looked up their address on my phone and I was on my way. I didn't care if she was still working or whatever, I still needed to see what the hell was going on. It was about thirty minutes away from our house; I made it there in 15. The place was pitch black. I called her phone again.

Instead of leaving I went around to the back to see if I seen any cars. As soon as I bent the corner right in the middle of the parking lot was Williams car. He was getting something out of the trunk. I waited for him to go back in, so I could follow him. What the hell was he up to? After he went in I did too. I wasn't sure exactly where he went, but I was sure as hell about to find out.

Chapter Nineteen: Secretes Revealed

Ж

As I tried to look out the tiny window at the top of the door, I couldn't see a thing. I wasn't sure how in the hell I was going to get out of here. William was fucking crazy, and I had to fucking find a way to escape or get him to let me leave. The only thing that came to my mind was to scream my way out.

"SOMEBODY HELP ME PLEASE! HELP ME PLEASE!" I yelled by the door. I didn't want to die in here. I started getting flash backs of when Mario beat the hell out of me. I couldn't let that happen again. "Someone please help me," I said again with my head against the door. That's when I heard someone coming. I hurried back to the bed just in case it was William. The door knob turned. I was terrified.

"Well, well, well; look who woke up from her nap," he said smiling from ear to ear. Then locked the door behind him.

"Can you please let me go?" I asked.

"Let you go? Let you go? No, I can't do that. You think it's of for you to play with peoples feeling like that? You think because your fine with a nice body that you can just fuck me and walk away?" he said angry. I slid all the way back into the corner.

"Look please just let me go. I'm sorry for what I did, I really am," I pleaded.

"You are far from Rio bitch. This is MIAMI BITCH, and you fucked with the wrong person!" he screamed. He then reached into his bag and pulled out a knife.

"Please William don't. I said I was sorry."

"Please William," he said mocking me. "You are going to learn that I have fucking feelings."

"William can we please just talk about this? I will leave Collin and be with you."

"Fuck Collin. I can have you right now," he said holding the knife to my face. "Oh yeah, your little boyfriend called for you too. I had to let him know that he wouldn't be seeing you anymore," he added. He then pressed the knife against my thigh. He started to cut at the skirt I had on to get if off. "As a matter of fact; I think I want a little taste before I get rid of you."

"Please I will do anything that you say, just let me go," I pleaded with him.

"I gave you that chance and you left. What you didn't think I was going to find out? You didn't think I had cameras in my fucking house to see everything that was going on? Na you didn't, your just a stupid little slut from Rio."

"William please, not like this. Untie me so that I can hold you and touch you," I said so he can free my hands.

"What do you think I'm stupid?"

"No baby, I just need to touch you that's all." I was hoping that he would have some kind of heart and untie me, but he just kept giving me this evil look. Then he began to untie my hands. "Thanks baby. You know I have to touch you while we are making love." As those words rolled off my tongue so did some vomit. I had to get free.

"Now so you won't try any funny business…" He tied my arms together from the front. "Now you can touch me all you want." He them took off my panties.

I began to cry. I knew that my life was over. I was never going to make it out of here. William was the one mistake I couldn't erase. Nobody was able to hear me, so no one would even know that I was in here. William climbed on top of me and he slid himself inside me. I just laid there.

"I'm going to have so much fun with you," he said as he was still inside me. This time I will make sure you won't get away."

"PLEASE JUST LET ME GO! JUST LET ME GO!" I begged and yelled.

"SHUT THE FUCK UP! YOUR NOT GOING ANYWHERE!" he yelled back following up by slapping me in the face. He still had the knife close by, and I was going to reach for it as soon as the time was right.

"WILLIAM PLEASE BABY LET ME GO! DON'T DO ME LIKE THIS, UNTIE ME!" And as soon as those words rolled off my tongue; the door flew open. My vision was still a little blurry, but the voice I heard was just what I needed to hear.

"GET THE FUCK OFF MY WOMAN!" Collin screamed as he hit William on the top of his head with a metal pipe. "Baby are you ok," he asked me picking me up of the mattress.

"Yes, how did you find me? I thought I was going to die in here."

"I read your note. I knew something was wrong when his ass called me," he said kicking William in the stomach.

We both hurried to get out of the building before William could catch up. As we were heading out the front door we heard the sirens going off. In that moment I knew where I needed to be Collin saved my life, and nothing on nobody would stop me for making things right between us.

"YOU STUPID BITCH!" William screamed; and then a loud pow sound went off. Collin looked at me and fell to the ground.

"NO!" I screamed trying to get him up. Over my head I heard six more-gun shots go off. When I looked up William was on the ground not moving. "COLLIN BABY WAKE UP!" I screamed again, but he still wants moving.

"Ma'am get out of the way. We got him," the paramedics said to me, as another one placed me on a stretcher.

"Is he going to be ok?" I asked in a panic.

"I'm not sure, lets get you to the hospital to get you checked out. You have some pretty nasty wombs."

I rode in that ambulance alone and worried. All because of me Collin got shot. All I could think about was; it should have been me.

Three Years Later

Sitting on the swing just thinking; I had a lot to thank god for. I was glad to be back home in Rio. Even though my parents are no longer here, I can still feel their love. The past few years was really rough for me. I had done a lot of things that I can say I'm not proud of. When I was in Miami, I saved up enough money for me to live comfortable, and I won a law suit from dealing with William. That day still brings me to tears.

Miami changed my life for the better and for the worse. William was killed that night from multiple gunshot wombs, but Collin. Collin never was the same again. He ended up having damage to his spine, and now he can no longer walk. The bullet that William shot into his back hit his spine and the fragments shattered. They weren't even able to retrieve them.

Collins parents were happy when they found out that we were moving back home, but them welcoming me wasn't so pretty. They blamed me for everything that happened to their son, which they should. I just wish they would forgive me. I was able to get a lot of his medical bills paid too. Turned out, William was in love with me so much that I was added to a lot of his legal papers. And since he is no longer living I got a large lump sum, plus I sued his company for falsifying documents that he had signed on my behalf.

Collin wasn't too happy with me once he recovered from his injuries. Nor was he happy about me being pregnant either. My daughter is almost two, Collins the father, but seeing how he can't walk nor play with her; he feels cheated. I tried my best to make him see the joy of everything, but he's still upset at me. His parents comes to pick up Camellia every weekend. I just wish we could be a family again.

Collin has a wife now and I guess he's happy. Things are what I call bitter sweet. I got what I deserved, but I also was blessed with a daughter that I can teach how to go about life the right way. When I look at her I see me, and I want her to know that karma is nothing to play with. As my mother always told me.

WHAT GOES AROUND ALWAYS COMES

BACK AROUND!

KARMA IS NOTHING BUT FIRE AND YOUR

BOUND TO GET BURNED!

THE END

Made in the USA
Middletown, DE
30 July 2022

70235704R00136